THE BLUE SKY OF SPRING

'You called on a lady called Miss Dryden-Smith,'
Nicholas's calm, icy explanation broke over the
other man's furious tones. 'She died of a heart
attack shortly after your visit. Immediately you
left the house, she began to make out a new
Will, leaving everything she had to a son nobody
had ever heard of. Nothing but gossip connects
you with the affair, but it's felt that something
might have taken place at the meeting to explain
her action. Her trustees would be glad to be able
to put to you one or two questions about the
interview you had with her.'

'I had no interview with her. I brought her a
parcel of pottery from America at the request of a
friend of mine. I gave it to her and she said
Thank you and Good-bye. . . . . If the information's
any use to you, you can use it.'

'Have you any objection to coming to Greenhurst
to see Miss Dryden-Smith's lawyer?'

Cliff, for the first time, hesitated.

The Blue Sky of Spring

Elizabeth Cadell

CORONET BOOKS
Hodder Paperbacks Ltd., London

Copyright © 1956 by Elizabeth Cadell
First published by Hodder and Stoughton Ltd. 1956
Coronet edition 1967
Third impression 1973

Printed in Great Britain
for Coronet Books, Hodder Paperbacks Ltd.,
St. Paul's House, Warwick Lane, London, EC4P 4AH
by Richard Clay (The Chaucer Press), Ltd.,
Bungay, Suffolk.

ISBN 0 340 00335 9

A blue sky of spring,
White clouds on the wing:
What a little thing
To remember for years—
To remember with tears!

WILLIAM ALLINGHAM: *A Memory*.

CHAPTER ONE

CLIFF HERMANN eased his big car round the curve of the narrow country road, came face to face with a farm cart, pulled up within a yard of it and prayed that he might soon find himself back on the wide stretches of an American highway.

English roads, he reflected bitterly, backing into the hedge, were fine for wagons or for horse-back riding—just fine—but for speedy, modern travel, they were jokes, and not funny ones. How those old-time coaches ever got along . . . but no; the coaches had not used these corkscrew lanes; they had kept to the main roads. They had been travelling, moreover, to places with names that people knew: Deal, Dover, Portsmouth, Bath. They were not, like himself, on the way to a small country town that nobody had ever heard of.

He had a strong impulse to turn and go back to London. He had telephoned before lunch to say that he would come down, but he had done so only because the weather had looked too bad to permit him to carry out any of his other engagements; though they had promised infinitely more enjoyment than this one, they had been out-of-doors, and the rain had been beating down with a steadiness that gave little hope for the rest of the day. But after lunch the rain had stopped; the sun had come out—and by that time it was too late to cancel his appointment to call upon this unknown Miss Dryden-Smith, at the obscure Hampshire market town of Greenhurst, with the parcel of Mexican pottery which, in a weak moment in New York, he had agreed to bring over and deliver to her while he was in England.

Well, here he was—almost. He would find this place,

Greenhurst; he would drive to the Red House, he would ask for Miss Dryden-Smith, he would hand over the parcel—which could and should have been posted—and then he would make his bow and depart.

He glanced at his watch : three-ten. He should be in Greenhurst by three-thirty; he determined to be out of it again by four. That would enable him to get back to London in time to salvage some of the entertaining projects he had been obliged to jettison.

He sketched, from his experience of English country hostesses, the pattern that his visit to the Red House would follow : Miss Dryden-Smith would say Won't you sit down and How interesting it is to meet someone all the way from America and How impossible it is, don't you know, to guess from an American's accent exactly whereabouts in America he comes from, and Would he care to see the garden, and Wouldn't he care for some tea, and Perhaps he knew that living in a house like this wasn't as pleasant as it had once been, because one couldn't get servants nowadays unless one paid them enormous wages, and——

And so on and so on.

Well, he would cut all that short—very short. He wasn't, at best, an over-friendly man; he would make quick work of this Miss Dryden-Smith's attempts to detain him.

He arrived at Greenhurst just before half-past three and recalled the directions he had been given : drive straight through Main Street—they called it High Street—take the left fork and look for a big, ugly red house standing a little way back from the road.

He got to the house and rang the bell. A deaf old man admitted him, led him through a large hall to the drawing-room, and ushered him into Miss Dryden-Smith's presence—and here Cliff's determination to resist hospitable pressure was checked by the realization that his hostess was not going to exert any. She was about as pleased to have him here, he saw at once, as he had been to come.

He looked at her tall, angular form and long face and decided that her expression was a degree less cordial than his own. Her manner was abrupt, her sentences brief and to the point. If he was irritated at having wasted the afternoon bringing down a valueless parcel of pottery, Miss Dryden-Smith was no less annoyed at having been compelled to remain at home in order to receive it.

'If I had known that it was going to turn out so fine,' she said at once, 'I would have asked you to come another day. But when you telephoned, it was raining and——'

'I'm sorry, but I couldn't have come down any other day,' said Cliff. 'I'm kind of busy trying to fit in a lot of business before I go back to the States. I've got quite a full programme.'

He had indeed. He was booked to fly back in ten days' time, and in the meantime he hoped to fit in five cocktail parties, two dinners, three dances, a race meeting and several theatres.

'What are you doing in England?' asked Miss Dryden-Smith, without any perceptible interest in her tone.

'I'm over here to talk about a play of mine that's to be put on in London in the autumn.' He stopped himself on the brink of telling her that Robert Debrett was to play the lead in it. If he mentioned Robert Debrett, her interest might be aroused—he did not think it would, but it might—and she would tell him what he already knew: that Robert Debrett had been married about a year ago in the Church whose spire was visible from these windows. Robert Debrett lived for a greater part of his time, not four miles away from Greenhurst. Robert Debrett had married Lucille Wayne, who . . .

He knew all that. Robert had told him. He wouldn't risk being told all over again by Miss Dryden-Smith.

'I don't know much about the theatre,' she told him. 'Music, yes; drama, no.'

She looked at him and took in his height and leanness, his thin, handsome face, his brooding look and his dark, almost angry looking eyes. She put his age down, accurately, as

thirty-five, and wondered fleetingly whether his unapproach-
able manner was due to bad temper or the desire to repel
too-eager advances.

'Did you drive down here?' she asked.

'Yes. Oh, you mean this?' He indicated the sling that supported one arm. 'That's all right. I can use the arm quite well;
I just let it rest up now and again.'

'How did you hurt it?'

He told her, and as she listened, she rose and walked to the
window and stood with her back to him, looking out at the
wet, glistening lawn. He thought it less than polite, but he was
not anxious to take up any more of her time, and said so.

'I only came down to give you the parcel—I hope the stuff
in it isn't damaged,' he said. 'I handled it as carefully as possible.'

'Thank you.' She turned from the window and faced him.
'Perhaps you will forgive me if I don't ask you to stay,' she
said. 'I feel . . . a little tired. My heart isn't strong.'

He thought, for a sardonic moment, that the words were an
excuse to get rid of him—and then he saw her face, and his
scepticism vanished. She looked white and drawn and, suddenly, very very old.

'If you're not feeling well,' he said, 'can I do anything? Call
anybody?'

'No, thank you. I shall be all right. But . . . you must forgive
me.'

'Of course.'

He bowed and went out, not without uneasiness, to his car.
She had looked . . . sick. He stood uncertainly, wondering
whether he ought to find the old man who had admitted him—
and then he saw a middle-aged woman going in through a side
gate, and watched her as she walked up to a door, opened it
with the familiarity of long usage and went inside.

He got into his car and drove away. Someone was there to
look after the old lady; there was no need for him to wait.

The visit had been even shorter than he had intended to

make it, and as he drove down the narrow, busy little High Street, he debated whether he should go straight back to London or whether he would keep a half-promise he had made to Robert Debrett when they had met in New York. Cliff had mentioned, casually, his errand in Greenhurst—and the name of the place had brought from the usually reticent Robert Debrett a flood of information and reminiscence regarding the family into which he had married, and whose home, Wood Mount, was a few miles from the town.

On a sudden impulse, Cliff took the turning that led him past the station and along the road which Robert had told him would lead to Wood Mount. A drive of some four miles brought him to the slope on which the house stood; he saw the gate, but the building itself was hidden and it was not until he had driven past it and climbed a steep side-road that he was able to look down and see through the trees the large, beautiful white house of which he had heard so much.

He switched off the engine and sat looking down through the foliage, and into his mind came all that Robert had told him. Here lived the Waynes—all six of them—in this house in which they had been born and brought up. It was odd to think of the celebrated, sophisticated Robert Debrett in this setting —and yet Robert had come, had fallen in love with Lucille Wayne, had married her and was now mooning over her between the performances of the play in which he was acting in New York.

New York—to Greenhurst. It was a long way, Sitting in this neck of the woods, mused Cliff, sitting here with nothing to listen to but the wind and the call of the birds; with nothing moving except the branches of the trees and that little squirrel over there . . . yes, it was a long, long way. New York was the present and this place . . . this must be one of those 'gleams of a remoter world' that—who was it, Shelley?—wrote about. Remote was the key-word.

Well, they could have it.

He had no intention of going to see the Waynes. The fulfil-

ment of the half-promise he had made to Robert could, he
thought, wait until his next visit to England. He was not
unduly interested in country life or in family life; he had noted
cautiously, as he listened to Robert, that though the three elder
Waynes were reasonably adult, the other three were in or near-
ing their teens; he had no great wish to encounter them.
Lucille, moreover, was expecting a baby; she would be in what
he termed an advanced stage, and though Robert's description
and proudly-displayed photographs of her proclaimed her
lovely, she could not be at her best at the moment, and she
would probably not be anxious to meet strangers. Next year,
perhaps, he would return with a present for the baby; it would
be rolling on a rug on the grass and he would bend over and
tickle its bare little stomach. But for the moment . . . No. No
Lucille. No Waynes.

He recalled other facts that he had learned from Robert.
The house—this unexpectedly lovely, graceful white house—
had been put up for sale about a year ago, after having been let
furnished for a time. Lucille Wayne had decided to sell
it—and her decision brought from afar, on the instant, un-
heralded, her scattered brothers and sisters, who came separ-
ately but remained to unite in a solid and unflinching front,
resolved to oppose the sale. Robert had seen their arrival;
Robert had stayed on to watch the subsequent struggle and in
the course of it had fallen in love with the turbulent, red-
haired Lucille. And now three separate units of the family
lived here in their self-contained flats: up, middle and down.
Cliff, his eyes on the house, tenanted each floor in turn. At the
top, Lucille, and, when he returned, Robert, and, when he
arrived, Robert junior. On the floor below, the sister next in
age to Lucille: what was her name? Roselle. That was it;
Roselle, who had married the young Greenhurst house-agent,
Jeff Milward. Roselle looked like a wild rose and had all a
wild rose's cooking skill. Jeff was sober and grave and wore his
wild rose proudly—and got one good meal a day by lunching
with his mother and father at Greenhurst.

That left the ground floor: here was where the three young ones lived, in the care of their brother Nicholas. Nicholas was . . . how old? He'd forgotten. Older than Roselle, who was twenty. So Nicholas was twenty plus whatever it was, and he was father and mother to the three young ones. Two boys and a girl. Julia—that was the the girl. Julia stayed in the mind, somehow. Julia was the little ugly one and all the other members of the family were—so Robert said—beautiful to behold. Julia, and two boys called something and something. And there was a dog, too.

Well, there they all were. Oh—and two outsiders who had attached themselves to the family at the same time in much the same way as Robert and who now worked as cook (Italian, male) and housekeeper (English, female) on the ground floor.

And it all sounded too, too fascinating, decided Cliff, but he hadn't the time to go into it. He would leave the Waynes in their leafy retreat, and he would high-tail it back to London to some more sophisticated entertainment. Robert would understand and forgive.

He switched on the engine, backed down the narrow lane and turned the car in the direction of London. If anybody had asked him, he would have said that he was putting Greenhurst and Wood Mount and the Waynes behind him for ever.

He would have been wrong.

CHAPTER TWO

JULIA WAYNE was bicycling to school, and bicycling fast. Few people who knew her well would have believed that she would pedal with such urgency when, at the journey's end, was an establishment she detested, and in which she spent so many long and unprofitable hours. But she was moving fast, and would liked to have moved still faster, for this was Thursday, and on Thursdays school had ceased to be the dreary and boring prospect that it remained on every other day of the week.

Getting educated, she thought as she covered the four miles between her home and the Greenhurst High School for Girls, was a very funny thing. They made you sit and swot over subjects that weren't the smallest use to you when you grew up. They droned on and on about x plus y equalling who cared what; they expected you to sort out gruesome and meaningless tongue-twisters like the square of the angles equalling the sum of the ones of the hypo ... hypot. ... Why did they teach all that stuff to girls? What good did it ever do them? Look at Lucille now: sitting up there on the top flat at home making a hash of knitting clothes for her baby that was coming, and dropping stitches and having to undo it all and start all over again, and why? Because when she was at school they'd wasted all her time on rubbish and never concentrated on things that she'd like to know about. Look at Roselle, married to Jeff Milward and living in the middle flat at home and not even being able to cook a decent meal without burning it to a frazzle and then sitting down and howling and starting all over again. Fat lot of good all those angles and triangles were to her now. Mathematics? Pah! History? Pooh! Botany, geology, geography? Keep the lot. Literature?

Literature ... now that was something. Literature was all right. You could understand why you had to pay attention when you were being taught about books and stories and poetry. You could see what it all meant. You could hear what it all meant. You could even feel what it meant—especially when Miss Dryden taught it to you.

Miss Dryden. . . .

She had only come for half a term while the literature mistress was away ill. She had been teaching at the school for less than two months; she would cease—oh, misery!—to teach there when the half-term holiday came round in a few days. The other mistress—oh, misfortune!—had got well again.

There was one crumb of comfort: Miss Dryden would not leave Greenhurst, because she lived there. But it was only a crumb. She would never again come into the classroom on Thursdays, bringing a sort of . . . a sort of radiance. Radiance, repeated Julia defiantly to the empty road. Yes, radiance. That hair, that sort of pale goldy hair. That face, shaped just like those books said—like a heart. Her eyes and her mouth—and her voice. Anybody could learn when people taught you in a voice that wasn't screechy and grating, but low and soft and lovely and even laughing. You could understand what words meant when she said them. You could hear the music behind the sentences, and even Shakespeare sounded all right suddenly—you wanted to read all the lines out loud and roll out the sounds and listen to them. You could love literature—when Miss Dryden taught you. Miss Dryden. . . .

At this point, Julia's thoughts became hazy. A vision of pale goldy hair rose before her and caused her to steer so close to the hedge that her satchel caught on a branch, held, dragged her off her bicycle and deposited her with her dreams into the ditch.

She got up, unhooked the satchel, righted the bicycle and went on her way. Her coat was muddy, her hat dented, her tie astray—but these were things Julia did not notice and did not worry about when they were brought to her notice.

She could not be said to be growing up gracefully. At eleven —nearly twelve—she had skinny legs, stringy red hair and a small freckled, far-from-lovely face. Her clothes lived a short, violent life; her grooming was at all times deplorable. Nobody in their senses would have posed her for a Learning-to-be-a-Beauty poster.

It was as well, perhaps, that she had, with regard to her person, an utter lack of self-consciousness. The only plain member of an outstandingly good-looking family, it was fortunate that comparisons occupied no part of her eager, busy little mind. She caught a glimpse of herself every morning in the mirror as she dashed a hair-brush over her hair and registered the fleeting thought that she looked gruesome—but life was too full—she decided—to worry about whether you looked like a monkey or whether you didn't. It didn't matter much until you grew up and wanted to stun some man into marrying you. For the moment, there was so much—so much. There was literature, and Miss Dryden standing up there against the blackboard with the light from the window catching her hair and making it look like a spider's web which the sun had touched in the early morning—only the web didn't have that golden sheen.

And to-day—to-day was Thursday and Thursday was the day when you had English prose in the morning and English grammar and composition in the afternoon. Two periods—two whole, blissful periods of Miss Dryden.

Julia's legs raced and her heart raced with them. School might be gruesome, on the whole—though this day-school in Greenhurst was better than being stuck day and night in that Convent, as she had been until last year, when they threw her out—but school with Miss Dryden was . . . it was almost bearable.

She reached school—as she did only on Thursdays—before the Late Bell sounded. She threw her bicycle into a shed with a hundred others, ran down to a basement cloakroom to change her shoes and then joined her Lower Third classmates for prayers in the main hall.

'You're early,' her friend, Lorraine, told her. 'For once.'

Julia waited, her heart throbbing with fear—but nothing more was said and she relaxed thankfully. One day they would guess; one day they would understand why she came early on Thursdays—but for the moment her secret was safe. Nobody knew—nobody suspected.

She mumbled the response to the prayers and stood silent as the hymn was sung. She would have liked to join in the singing —especially to-day—but by popular request she refrained. Her voice, she liked to think, was somewhat too individual for community singing.

She prepared, with the others, to march to her classroom, but the Headmistress halted the school.

'I have something to say to the Lower Third form,' she said. 'You will join the Upper Third for arithmetic this morning and the Lower Fourth in the gymnasium this afternoon. There will be no English periods to-day as Miss Dryden will not be able to come to school,' She paused. 'I am sorry to tell you that her aunt, Miss Dryden-Smith, died suddenly yesterday afternoon.'

There was a buzz and a murmur, stilled instantly by the Headmistress.

'Silence,' she requested. 'That is all.'

Julia, standing stricken, was pulled to attention by Lorraine and brought back to the dreary present. No literature. No Miss Dryden. Nothing. Nothing but gym and arithmetic. It would——

Lorraine clutched her arm as they turned in the direction of the gymnasium.

'That's what I was going to tell you, only there wasn't time,' she said. 'Did you know?'

'No,' said Julia, and might have added that she did not care. She knew Miss Dryden-Smith, and she had been to her house, but she thought her, in the main, a bad-tempered old woman who objected to girls hitting tennis balls into her grounds—as though anybody had any control over a tennis ball. She was dead, which was awful in a way, but then she was old, and old people did die—but it was a pity she had died . . . it was a pity she hadn't waited until after Thursday. . . .

When school was over, Julia decided that she would not go straight home; she would go to the High Street and look in on Uncle Bill Milward, who would be able to tell her if Miss Dryden would be coming back to school before the half-term holiday. She was not certain what Mr. Milward had to do with Miss Dryden-Smith, but she knew that it was something which kept him in touch with her affairs—and therefore with Miss Dryden.

She found her sister Roselle's husband, Jeff Milward, in the house agent's office which he and his father ran in the High Street. He lifted his steady grey eyes from his work and studied her briefly. She would have been appalled to know that he knew quite well why she was there. Her heart, closed to her schoolmates, was no mystery to the older members of her family. Jeff well knew her feelings for Miss Dryden. He was also aware that her brother Nicholas shared them.

He smiled his slow smile.

'Well, what brings you here?' he asked.

'I wanted to see Uncle Bill to ask him about Miss Dryden-Smith. She's dead, isn't she?'

'She is, I'm sorry to say. She died suddenly yesterday after-noon.'

'Why suddenly?' Julia sat on the edge of his desk and pushed back her school hat until it hung by its elastic. 'Didn't anybody know she was going to?'

'No.'

'But I thought she had a weak heart, and would've gone off suddenly in any case?'

'Her heart wasn't strong, but so long as she didn't over-exert herself, she was all right.'

'Did she go and over-exert herself?'

'Not as far as anybody knows. She had a very quiet after-noon—but the attack came on suddenly.'

'And she died?'

'Yes. And now how about going home to tea and keeping out of the way and not bothering anybody, and minding your own business? Or, alternatively, going across the road and wasting Nicholas's time instead of mine or my father's?'

Julia glanced through the window at the large newly-painted notice on the other side of the street: GREENHURST TRAVEL AGENCY and, in smaller letters, *Nicholas Wayne*.

'He doesn't like me to go in,' she explained. 'He says——'

'I know what he says. He says he's busy. Well, I'm busy

too,' said Jeff. 'So you'd better go off home. And tell Roselle, will you, that I might be late.'

'Why will you? Do you have to do extra work because of Miss Dryden-Smith?'

'Yes. My father is one of her Trustees; Mr. Wylie is the other. That won't mean anything to you,' said Jeff, 'and I can't stop to explain.'

'She had an awful lot of money, hadn't she?'

'She had a great deal.'

'And now . . .' Julia hesitated, but she had to know. 'And now Miss Dryden'll get it, won't she?'

Jeff seemed to hesitate for a moment and then:

'Yes; she'll get it,' he said.

'And then, I suppose . . . I mean, she won't teach any more, will she?'

'She won't need to work if she doesn't want to.'

'Will she want to, do you think?'

'Why don't you ask her?'

'Because . . . it's sort of rude, isn't it?'

'Very. And now get off my desk,' ordered Jeff, 'and go home.'

She went disconsolately out of the office and stood hesitating. She wanted to go across the road to see Nicholas, but Nicholas had a short way with her when she disturbed him at his work. But this was an occasion on which she must take a risk or two. She crossed the road and opened the office door cautiously, and her brother looked up briefly.

'Shut the door as you go out,' he said.

'I only want to ask you something,' pleaded Julia.

'Well, ask me when I get home to-night.'

'But it's sort of important.'

'It'll keep. On your way home, you might collect those things I left at the cleaners. Here's the ticket. And tell Pietro I'll be late.'

At the mention of Pietro, Julia's heart lifted a little. The girls at school might think it was odd to have an Italian working as cook for the family, and certainly Pietro looked odd enough—but when it came to collecting scraps of information that eluded everybody else, Pietro had no equal. He would know how long teachers had to stay away when their aunts died. If he didn't know, he would find out.

She closed the door, and Nicholas, at his desk, gave a smile that was half derision and half pity. Poor little devil—she wanted to know how long Estelle Dryden would be away from school and she was using her small store of cunning to find out without giving away the secrets of her little heart.

The secrets of the heart. At least, thought Nicholas, his own heart held no secrets. He loved Estelle and he wanted to marry her. She knew it, and so, probably, did everybody else in Greenhurst. He had wanted to marry her ever since the day, almost a year ago, when they had met on his return from his period of National Service. He did not understand how, having known her throughout his life, having grown up in the same town, he could look at her one bright summer's day and know, suddenly and without preparation, that he loved her and wanted to make her his wife; but that was how it had happened, and his life had changed and become fuller and brighter and infinitely deeper, and Estelle's name hummed in his mind throughout his waking hours, and her face came to him in his dreams at night.

And there were only two obstacles in his path. The first was her aunt's thirty thousand pounds, which were now hers and which he would rather be without but which he did not intend to treat as an insurmountable hurdle. The second ... the second was something he could do nothing about. God had created him—two years too late. He was Estelle's junior by two years—and he knew that, like all women, Estelle would have preferred to be two years younger and not two years older than her husband.

He regretted his insufficient years more bitterly than she could do—but he knew that at twenty-two he was a good deal more mature than most men of his age. He was running a home and he was supporting his two younger brothers and sister, Simon and Dominic and Julia. His brother-in-law, Robert Debrett, had offered to help; Jeff and his father were willing to assist, but he had wanted to see if he could run his own part of the house on his own earnings—and he had succeeded. There was no margin—but there were no debts. People had said that he was ill-advised to open a travel agency in a small place like Greenhurst—but he had opened it and it was thriving. It was thriving. It was paying. It was growing. His capital would grow with it. He could support Estelle with, or preferably without, her aunt's fortune. If she would marry him, they would live at Wood Mount and add their own family to the existing one.

If she would marry him. . . .

He picked up the receiver and dialled a number.

'Estelle? Nicholas. When can I see you?'

'I . . . I don't know.' Her voice held an odd note.

'This evening?'

'Yes. But Nicholas, there's something——'

'Hold it. Someone's coming in. Oh—it's only Jeff.'

'Thank you,' said Jeff. 'Is that Estelle you're talking to?'

'Yes.'

'Then ring off. I've got something to tell you.'

'He says he's got something to tell me,' Nicholas told Estelle. 'Would you like to listen to it?'

'I know it already,' she said, and rang off.

Nicholas looked at the receiver in surprise for a moment and then replaced it.

'She went away,' he said. 'I wish people wouldn't interrupt me when I'm talking to my future wife.'

Jeff studied his brother-in-law with the long, deliberate stare which, Nicholas thought, made him look so much like his father.

'You're so sure about this?' he asked, at last.

'Sure? Of course I'm not sure,' said Nicholas. 'I'm just

hanging on to a thread of hope, that's all. Cigarette?'

'Thanks. Perhaps if Estelle hadn't lived here most of her life,' said Jeff, accepting a light and sitting on the desk, 'you'd have found it easier. You look a lot more than twenty-two and she looks a lot less than twenty-four—but when you've grown up together in the same narrow little circle, the——'

'I know; the difference in age gets etched in over the years. She can remember a damn sight too much about the old days. She can remember holding my head after I'd over-eaten at one of her own parties. She was twelve then—Julia's age—and I was ten.'

'Dominic's age,' commented Jeff.

'Yes. I only hope I looked as handsome. But I doubt it. Estelle remembers a whole lot about the old days that I'd rather she'd forgotten. For years and years she's been used to thinking of herself as Lucille's friend—and me as the younger brother. It isn't a good platform for romance.'

'I suppose not. Did Estelle tell you anything about her aunt just now?'

'No. What about her?'

'I mean, did she mention her aunt's will?'

'No. Why? Any sensational last minute change?'

Jeff hesitated, and Nicholas stared at him.

'Well, come on, come on,' he urged, at last, 'was there or wasn't there?'

'There ... wasn't,' said Jeff. 'But——' He broke off. 'I suppose you know I shouldn't be telling you this?'

'Do you think I'm going to yell the information up and down the High Street?'

'No. If I'm any judge,' said Jeff, slowly, 'you won't have to spread the news; I'm willing to bet that the whole of Green-hurst will know the entire story before to-night's out.'

'Did she disinherit Estelle?'

'She was going to.'

'I ... I don't understand,' said Nicholas, slowly.

'Neither does anybody else,' said Jeff. 'But the fact is that shortly before she died, Miss Dryden-Smith wrote out part of a new Will. Only . . . she didn't live to finish it.'

There was a silence for some time.

'Tell me,' said Nicholas, breaking in at last.

'Yesterday afternoon,' said Jeff, 'she had a visitor—nobody knows who it was or anything about him. Chap with a parcel. He came, and he went. After he had gone, the housekeeper, Mrs. Ambler, came in and found Miss Dryden-Smith in the drawing-room, desperately ill with one of her heart attacks. She told Mrs. Ambler, as well as she was able to tell her, that she was to bring her husband in and they—the husband and wife—were to witness something. When Mrs. Ambler hurried back with her husband, Miss Dryden-Smith was . . . dead.'

'And the Will . . . it wasn't witnessed?'

'It wasn't even completed. But it was clear enough—as far as it went.'

'And how far did it go?'

'She left everything of which she died possessed to . . . her son.'

Nicholas stared across the desk in stupefaction, and his brother-in-law waited patiently for him to speak.

'I . . . I don't . . . What son?' asked Nicholas, in a dazed voice.

'You may well ask. It was a hell of a shock to poor old Wylie—my father's been plying him with stimulants at intervals since yesterday to settle his nerves. I don't know which is upsetting his lawyer's mind most—the idea of his spinster client suddenly producing an offspring out of the hat, or the fact that the Amblers couldn't very well help reading the paper—and can't really be expected to keep news of that kind to themselves. It's getting round; you can tell from the excitement in the shops that rumours are beginning to circulate already.'

'To her . . . her *son*?' repeated Nicholas, in an incredulous voice.

'Her son. I've seen the paper. The writing, as far as it went, was firm enough—and only too clear. "I leave all of which I died possessed to my son. . . ." '

'And then—she died?'

'And then she died.'

'Is there . . . *can* there be?'

'How can anybody tell? My father and Mr. Wylie have been turning over the possibilities ever since they saw the sheet of paper and the words written on it, but they're not getting any nearer to a solution. It's impossible for them—come to that, it's impossible for anybody to think of Estelle's aunt—the rigid, uncompromising Miss Dryden-Smith—as a woman with a past!'

'Must she have had a past? I mean, couldn't she have written the words under some kind of . . . delusion?'

'She was clear-headed enough when she spoke to Mrs. Ambler. She was ill; very ill. She was gasping and in great pain, but she was issuing clear enough orders. As Mrs. Ambler left the drawing-room, she was already beginning to write.'

'And Estelle——'

'She was at school, of course, when it all happened; she saw her aunt at lunch, and that was the last time she saw her alive. Mrs. Ambler put a call through to her at once—as well as to my father and Mr. Wylie. They all got there together—but the Amblers already knew, unfortunately, what had been written on the paper. If they hadn't seen it, there might have been some hope of keeping the thing quiet. They said, of course—at least, Mrs. Ambler said; the old man was too deaf to follow much of what was going on—that they wouldn't let a word of anything pass their lips, but——'

'No,' said Nicholas, thoughtfully. 'No. It would be expecting too much. Mrs. Ambler's a decent woman, but she's a notorious gossip.'

'Well, I've told you,' Jeff got to his feet. 'Odd business, isn't it? If God had given her a few more minutes. she would have signed away everything that she brought Estelle up to believe would be hers after her death.'

Nicholas followed him to the door, and they stood looking out into the sunny little street.

'See the bunch in the grocer's,' commented Nicholas. 'Heads close together and tongues going sixteen to the dozen. What does Estelle say about it all? No, don't tell me; I'm going out to see her. I'll ask her myself. She never really wanted to come into all her aunt's money, but I don't suppose she thought of anything like this.'

'Who did?' asked Jeff, as he moved away.

CHAPTER THREE

NICHOLAS closed his office and went to the Red House, walking up the drive with a caution engendered by years of stormy encounters with its owner. Then he remembered that the owner was dead; now and henceforward he could walk boldly up, scrunching the gravel firmly beneath his feet, without fear that an upper window would be thrown open and a crisp voice order him to take himself round to the side door and not to pollute the hall with his muddy shoes. Miss Dryden-Smith seemed to have an extra sense that told her when visitors were approaching the house; her greeting was seldom cordial and, in the case of Nicholas and his contemporaries, had sometimes bordered on the threatening.

She had known quite well, lately, why he had come to the house so often. The thought came to Nicholas as he reached the house that perhaps this knowledge might have had something to do with her attempt to change her Will; it was a remote possibility, but perhaps she had thought, towards the end, of fortune hunters; perhaps she had made some hasty plan to protect her niece.

He said as much to Estelle when they had walked out to the

little summer-house in which they had so often met—out of sight of the windows, safe from her aunt and her sudden swoops, her keen eyes and caustic tongue. He had taken Estelle's hand in his and was holding it, as he loved to do, against his cheek. It was one of the few privileges she allowed him; it was not much, thought Nicholas, but it was better than nothing.

'Could she have decided to put her fortune a bit more out of range of mercenary applicants for your hand? Was she putting up hurdles, as they did in fairy stories, between the hopeful suitors and the princess?'

'It sounds . . . far-fetched,' said Estelle.

'Yes, but so does the whole story of her end. Did you quarrel with her?'

'No. I think I must be the one person in Greenhurst who didn't.' Estelle spoke dreamily. 'I've thought, lately, that quarrelling was nothing more than her favourite hobby. She loved skirmishing. She's carried on a grumbling war in this town for more than thirty years, and I think she enjoyed every minute of it. She used different methods to irritate different people—it was an art. She liked to watch victims growing red in the face and beginning to splutter—while she herself remained cool and self-possessed and thoroughly sensible. Perhaps that was really the secret of her effect on people—her combination of sound sense and tactlessness.'

'Was it sound sense that moved her when she began to write that Will?'

She looked at him thoughtfully.

'Nicholas, have you made up your mind that there couldn't have been a son?'

'I'm open to conviction—but it doesn't tie up with the picture we've all had of her all these years,' said Nicholas. 'I can't make a cool summary of her character when she's lying dead up in that room, but nobody, not even you, Estelle darling, could associate her with any of the tender passions.'

'She wasn't always sensible and middle-aged; Uncle Bill

says that, when she was young, she was a remarkably hand-some girl.'

Like the Waynes, she gave Mr. Milward a relationship that he could not in fact claim. But, like them, she had known him for a great part of her life and, like them, she had put him in the place of a father she couldn't remember.

'How did you feel'—Nicholas left her side and walked to the door of the summer-house and stood leaning against it—'how did you feel when you realized that if she'd completed the new Will and signed it and had it witnessed, you——'

'I would have been left with nothing?'

'Yes.'

'I've got a profession—and a job. It seems extraordinary to remember how strongly she opposed them both. That's what's . . . that's what I find the most puzzling part of the whole thing—the fact that she could go back, at the end, on so much of her own advice and argument. When I decided to work for a degree, she thought I was behaving absurdly; she pointed out that I'd never need a profession or a job and that I was only going to train for one in order to annoy her. She was absolutely without any thought, then, of ever changing her Will. I can't make you understand why I'm so certain—but I feel quite sure that even up to the last day—yesterday—when she was talking to me at lunch . . . even then, she had no idea of doing what she did. What she so nearly did. Something happened after that— I'm certain of it.'

'You mean that it was something to do with this man who came to see her?'

'It . . . it looks like it, doesn't it?'

'Who was he?'

Estelle shook her head helplessly.

'Nobody knows. Nobody has the faintest idea who he is or why he came. Unless it was simply to bring a few pieces of pottery.'

'Wasn't there any note of his appointment in your aunt's diary?'

'None. He telephoned before lunch. He came—and he went.'

She came across to stand beside him, and he looked down at her soberly. Looking up she saw his eyes and wondered secretly, humbly, why he loved her so much.

She was a girl with singularly little vanity. Perhaps the years with her aunt, who did not pay compliments, had robbed her of a little confidence. She knew that men, other than Nicholas, had found her desirable, and had wondered at the freakish chance that drew them to her when there had been available women with more beauty and more charm. She looked at her reflection long and soberly and saw that her hair was coarse, her skin far from the dazzling fairness that she had so envied in Roselle Milward; her mouth was too large, her eyes too small, her nose a mere nothing. She did not know that the hair curled itself into tight little tendrils of gold, into which a man longed to slip his fingers, her skin had a clear glow and was as soft as silk; her eyes gleamed with curiosity or amusement or—now and then—with a swift uprush of anger. She was slim with a boyish grace; she had good sense and good understanding—and an elusiveness that Nicholas Wayne found baffling.

'What happened yesterday?' he asked.

'I saw her for the last time—alive—at lunch. It was raining, and she said she was expecting a visitor. She didn't say who it was, and I didn't ask. When I was younger, I used to fall into the trap and ask and get snubbed for my pains—so I didn't ask her who was coming. After lunch, I went back to school and she went into the drawing-room. She sent Mrs. Ambler out to change her library book, and said that she wished she hadn't agreed to see anybody because it had turned out such a lovely afternoon.'

'Was she quite well?'

'Yes. Mrs. Ambler went out, and told her husband to keep a look out for the visitor. He's too deaf to hear the bell, but he saw a man arrive and let him in. He says he didn't see him go.

Mrs. Ambler didn't see him at all. There was a car standing in the drive when she got back—she caught a glimpse of it as she went in by the side door, but she imagined the visitor was still in the drawing-room. As she got into the house, she heard the car drive away, and so she went to the drawing-room with the library books, and then she—she saw Aunt Mary standing at the window clinging to it and looking like . . . like death.'

Nicholas put an arm round her and she leaned against him and went on speaking quietly.

'Mrs. Ambler helped her over to the sofa and rushed to the drawer of the bureau for her heart pills. Aunt Mary took them —that is, she took them from Mrs. Ambler, but she wouldn't stop to let her open the box and take them out, as she usually did. She lay there for a few moments and then she told Mrs. Ambler to fetch her husband because she wanted them to sign a paper. She pointed, and Mrs. Ambler brought her paper and a pen, and she was writing, she said, as she went out. It only took a moment to fetch her husband—she didn't even stop to explain matters to him because he's too deaf to have taken them in quickly. She just took him along to the drawing-room —and they found Aunt Mary . . . and the sheet of paper with the writing on it.'

There was a pause, and Nicholas broke into it with a question.

'You mentioned the parcel that was brought by this man. Didn't that give any sort of indication—any address?'

'None. It was unopened, and it was nothing but another of the additions to her collection, sent by the people who've sent her similar parcels, on and off, for years.'

'No connection with the Will?'

'None. They're people Mr. Wylie told her about; she'd never heard of them. They're simply business people she wrote to when Mr. Wylie told her they might have occasional things to interest her. The parcels usually came by post, but once or twice they've been brought by people coming over. But this time, she didn't open the parcel, which makes it look somehow as though the man had two objects in coming to see her—the obvious one to bring the parcel, and the other, the news that ... that in a way, killed her.'

'What does Uncle Bill think about it all?' enquired Nicholas, after a time.

'He doesn't know what to think, though he's doing his best to find some sort of explanation. Poor old Mr. Wylie has more or less collapsed; I think that in all his sixty-odd years of practice, none of his spinster clients ever claimed a son. Uncle Bill's looking after everything.'

'Does he believe in this son?'

'He won't rule him out. He thinks it might be something to do with the man who came—he feels that he might have brought some message, even some kind of demand. We'll probably never know.' She frowned. 'But if the new Will had been completed, Nicholas, where could we have begun to look for him? Uncle Bill says they would have put notices in newspapers, but that doesn't sound very effective—how do they know he'd ever have seen the notices?'

'She travelled a lot, didn't she, once?'

'She spent much more time abroad than she did in England —until her heart began to give trouble and she had to stay at home. But for years she went all over the world—and that was the time when, according to Uncle Bill, she was a very handsome woman.'

'A very handsome—and very rich—girl, spending long periods abroad. It opens up a big field,' said Nicholas, thoughtfully. 'There was a larger staff here in the old days— would any of them still be living in Greenhurst?'

'Even if they were, what could they tell us? That she was in South America in the year this, or in Spain or France or Germany in the year that? She used to stay abroad for a year or two at a time.'

'Then there might indeed be a son.'

'There is a son,' said Estelle, with the utmost conviction.

He glanced down at her curiously.

'Go on,' he invited.

'Before there was a son,' said Estelle, in the same tone of certainty, 'there was a husband.'

'Because why?'

'Because I'm prepared to swear that if Aunt Mary had ever fallen in love—and I hope she did—she would have given her heart but kept her head. Do you agree?'

Nicholas nodded. This was no time to voice his conviction that no man would ever have succeeded in bowling over Miss Dryden-Smith. Like the little figures with weighted feet, she would have swayed this way or that, but she would never have toppled over. Her natural position was an upright one.

'If there was a husband,' he said, 'and if the son was, therefore, what might be called open and above-board, why the long years of secrecy?'

'I don't know. I can't even begin to guess—but I knew her as well as anybody in this world, and certain facts about her stand out like landmarks. One of her strongest instincts was to keep her money in the family. She brought me here when my parents died simply because she wanted me to be brought up among the Dryden heirlooms and the Smith money. They were to be mine, she always told me, because I was a Dryden and for no other reason. It was then that she added Dryden to Smith and became Dryden-Smith. I was—so she said—the next in succession, and she told me all my life how desirable it was, if it was at all possible, to keep family money and possessions safe to be passed from hand to hand as a sort of trust down through succeeding generations. She believed that it was good citizenship—a steady, sober, rooted way of life. You didn't hoard, you didn't dissipate—you received, you used to good purpose and you handed on. She was always glad that I was there to inherit everything. The thought of dying without a close and direct heir would have made her miserable. And that's why I'm absolutely certain that there's a son. I can't tell you why she didn't make a Will in his favour long ago. Perhaps she thought he was dead. Perhaps she didn't know where he was. Perhaps this man who came to see her brought news of some kind. Whatever he said to her, he must have convinced her that there was somebody who had a stronger claim to her possessions than I had—and when he left the house she made up her mind that she would leave him all she had.'

'This visitor—did *nobody* know anything about him?'

'No; nobody.'

'He didn't walk here. This car—didn't anybody see the number-plate?'

'No. Mrs. Ambler caught that one glimpse of it and nothing more. Old Ambler saw it when he let the man in, but all he knows is that it was black.'

'Very helpful. Could he make a guess at the fellow's age?'

'Between thirty and forty, he thought. But he did notice one thing, and that was that the man had his arm in a sling.'

'That doesn't help much.'

'It might; he says that the sling was the same colour as Mrs. Ambler's second-best summer frock.'

'And what colour's that?'

'Navy blue with a sort of squiggly pattern in white.'

'Then the puzzle's solved,' said Nicholas. 'All you have to do is to go out looking for a man in a black car with his arm in a blue sling with a squiggly pattern of white. Simplicity itself.'

'That's what I thought,' said Estelle.

He looked at her and spoke broodingly.

'A few more minutes of life, and your aunt would have left you poor,' he said. 'And I'm sorry—in one way—that she didn't live to do it. Because then we would have been on more equal terms, you and I. Now you're the wealthy Miss Dryden —but I'd like you to know that in spite of that, I love you very much indeed.'

She put a hand lightly on his arm.

'You're very sweet, Nicholas,' she said.

'I love you,' he said, steadily. 'Just keep on remembering that. This isn't the time to talk about it, and I won't worry you

until—until things get straightened out here. But you'll remember, won't you?'

'Yes. I'll remember.'

'And now I've got a message from Lucille. She wants me to
bring you out to Wood Mount.'

Estelle shook her head.

'I can't, Nicholas. I'll go out and see her as much as I can,
but I've got to be here—at any rate, until after the funeral.
I'm staying with the Milwards here in Greenhurst, and then
I'll be on hand if I'm wanted for anything. I'd be too much out
of the way if I stayed with Lucille.'

'Are you going to Uncle Bill's now?'

'Yes.'

'Then I'll take you there. I'm not going to leave you in this
house by yourself.'

'The Amblers are here. But I'm glad to be away . . . for the
moment. . . .'

They walked slowly to the house and Nicholas waited while
Estelle went upstairs to get ready. Walking slowly from one
room to the other, it seemed to him that Miss Dryden-Smith's
tall, spare form was following him. Once or twice he thought
he saw her in the shadowed corners of a room, and it seemed to
him that she was waiting for something. But what it was, he
could not tell.

CHAPTER FOUR

NICHOLAS got to Wood Mount about seven o'clock that
evening and carried out his usual practice of visiting his sisters
to catch up on the domestic news of the day. He began, as
always, by going up to Lucille's flat on the top floor.

Lucille was sitting on a chair by a window that overlooked

the lawn. Nicholas greeted her briefly, studied the garment she was knitting and passed judgment.

'Too small,' he said.

She raised her lovely face to his and smiled.

'Perhaps,' she agreed, 'but that's because I'm trying to knit more tightly. The last thing I made looked like a fishing net. I'm beginning to think that Julia's right about education—too much preoccupation with the wrong subjects.'

'Or not enough follow-through. If they'd linked your biology lessons with a few hints on how to clothe the results of your biological urges——'

'Oh, don't call him that!' begged Lucille. 'He might hear you and be born looking like the result of a biological urge. Do you have to reduce my passion for Robert to those terms?'

'Sorry. Velly solly.'

'Nicholas——'

'Well?'

'There are some odd rumours going round about Miss Dryden-Smith.'

'Have they got as far as this? Well, I suppose it's not surprising,' commented Nicholas, sitting down and helping himself to a cigarette. 'Jeff came to the office and let me into a big secret—but the whole of the High Street seemed to be discussing the news. What does rumour say?'

'That Miss Dryden-Smith left all her money to ... it sounds fantastic ... to her son. And that Estelle gets nothing.'

'Any more?'

'Lots; a mysterious stranger—a man—came to see her yesterday just before she died. He had a trunk with him. Ambler let him in but he crept out again and left Miss Dryden-Smith on the drawing-room floor, unconscious. His arm was bandaged. The general idea seems to be that he's the son and heir. I know it's all quite wild, but there must be something underneath it all. What's the truth?'

'She did begin to make a new Will.'

Lucille dropped her knitting and stared at him.

'You mean . . . leaving out Estelle?'

'Yes.'

'Had they—quarrelled?'

'No. There's no explanation—unless it can be supplied by the man who came to see her. I think Uncle Bill and old Wylie would like to put their hands on him and ask him a few questions, but he appears to have come out of the blue and gone back into it without trace.'

'Where's Estelle?'

'At Uncle Bill's. She's staying there until the funeral's over. I asked her to come out here, but I didn't press it—it's better for her to be in Greenhurst while there's so much business for her to see to.'

'When is the funeral to be?'

'The day isn't fixed, but it'll be pretty soon. After that Estelle will be pretty busy clearing up things at the house.'

'She's finished that teaching job at the school, hasn't she?'

'Yes—and I'm sorry.'

'Because of Julia?'

'Yes. Believe it or not, Lu, she was actually working. She's actually been sitting down night after night—unasked—doing her homework. She'd fetched a lot of her less-read books down from the attic—Shakespeare among them—and she sits up in bed at night giving out poetry by the stanza until I go in and stop her. And it's all for Estelle. And now that there won't be any more Estelle at school, who's to say that Julia Wayne's going to keep it up?'

'Well, don't worry; wait and see. Perhaps Estelle has planted the seed, and perhaps the ground isn't as stony as you think it is.'

'I hope not. You're lucky in one way, Lu; you won't be expected to turn up at the funeral.'

'Poor Miss Dryden-Smith,' said Lucille, softly. 'I can't imagine Greenhurst without her. Do you know what she called me once?'

'Bossy. And so you were.'

'She said I was an over-riding female. Coming from her, I thought that was funny.'

'But strictly accurate.'

'I shall never be allowed to forget it.'

Nicholas rose and stubbed out his cigarette.

'Well, I'm going down. I wonder what happened to that fellow.'

'What fellow?'

'The one Robert said he'd asked to look us up.'

'Perhaps he forgot. I can't say I'm sorry. Who wants to meet strange men looking like this?'

' "Who, looking like this, wants to meet strange men",' corrected Nicholas. 'If I saw a man looking like this, I'd think he was very strange indeed.'

'And I'd feel very sorry for him, because I'd know how bulky and uncomfortable he was feeling. When do Simon and Dominic get home for their half-term, Nicholas?'

'They'll be here at the end of the week.'

'I'd like to be here to see them—but I hope the baby'll be here before then. How long do they get?'

'Only three days. Julia gets a whole week! He groaned. 'A whole week of Julia! Thank heaven I've got an office to retreat to. Well, so long, Lu; if the baby starts in the night, thump on the floor and maybe Jeff'll hear you and let me know.'

'Thank you very much. He'd have to do more than thump to wake you.'

Nicholas went to the floor below and looked warily into his sister Roselle's flat. Experience had taught him that anybody going in when she was engaged in any kind of work found himself taking it from her and doing it more efficiently. In justice, he was bound to admit that she did not seek aid; but there was something about her air of utter unhandiness that drove onlookers to action. Her efforts to run her little home made Nicholas think of a pretty little Shetland pony trying to draw a plough.

He closed the door, wrinkled his nose, sniffed and came to the conclusion that Jeff was coming home to feast upon charred chicken. He walked into the kitchen and found Roselle flushed with exertion and tearful with worry.

'What's up? Meal all gone to pot?' he enquired.

'It . . . it looks h-horrible,' said Roselle.

'Smells horrible, too.' Nicholas lifted a saucepan lid and peered in. 'I'd call that a total loss if I were you.'

'It isn't as if I didn't try,' said Roselle, bleakly. 'I do every single thing the book says.'

'Well, why worry? Rome wasn't starved in a day,' Nicholas reminded her. 'And Jeff's got a digestion like a horse. Why don't you let Miss Cornhill come up and give you a hand?'

Roselle shook her head.

'No. It's nice of you to offer, but if I don't learn now, I'll go on being useless all my life.'

Nicholas looked at her. In these last months, she had lost none of her gentle flower-like beauty, but there was a wistful look in her eyes. She had no gift for home-making; she worked hard, but none of the rooms in the flat looked cared-for. She pored over cookery books and shed tears over steaming saucepans, and then set before her husband food that Nicholas, with unbounded admiration, watched him eat without complaint. He wondered sometimes if Jeff ever remembered David Copperfield and his Dora; it must, he thought, be comfortless living, however deeply Jeff's eyes glowed when they rested on his lovely young wife.

'Have you seen Estelle?' Roselle asked.

'Yes. I saw her this evening.'

'How is she?'

'All right; a bit bewildered.'

'Is it true about somebody calling on her aunt and telling her he was her son?'

'No. Or again, yes. This mystery is one of *cherchezing* the *homme* and not, for once, trying to find the female.'

'Poor man. . . .'

'Why? To have had Miss Dryden-Dragonsmith for a mother?'

'No. And she's dead,' Roselle reminded him gently. 'I said poor man because he might have liked to know that she had remembered him—at the end. He's poorer to-day, whoever he is, by all those thousands of pounds. I'm glad Estelle didn't lose them all, but I wish the son had been able to share some of the money.'

'Well, perhaps he'll turn up one day. Look—if your dinner's gone wrong, why don't you bring Jeff downstairs to share ours?'

'No.' Roselle shook her head. 'I have to go on trying, Nicholas.'

And Jeff, thought Nicholas, going downstairs to his own superbly-cooked meal, Jeff has to go on starving.

He went to his room. The house was quieter with the two boys away at school, but no house which contained Julia could be peaceful. He could hear her now in the bath, singing loudly and tunelessly, and he marvelled once more at her talent for picking up collectors' gems. Her latest, now being performed in the bathroom, was a song beginning:

> Count Blunderbuss arose one day
> And said unto fair Lady May.

And presently she would go downstairs and pick out on the piano, with one finger, a melody to which she would sing in what she believed was an Irish accent:

> Oi'm a daycent buoy from Oireland, deny it no man can,
> Oi'm no harum-scarum, devil-may-carum LOW BORN
>   Oirish MAN.

And some people's children, reflected Nicholas, undressing and preparing to blast his sister out of the bathroom, played little rippling pieces by Bach, or recited Hail to thee, blithe Spirit, bird thou never wert.

'Come on—out you come,' he ordered, thundering upon the bathroom door.

'Oh, Nicholas,' came Julia's eager voice. There was a splash, a plop, a padding across the floor and the door was flung open to reveal a pink, dripping, unabashed Julia. 'Oh, Nicholas, you know what? I've got something terribly important to tell you! Miss——'

'Look, would you mind draping a towel round your totally exposed torso when you want to hold a conversation with an adult member of the opposite sex?' requested Nicholas.

'What's the harm?' said Julia, indignantly. 'You're only my brother.'

'You're almost twelve years of age, and it's time you retreated behind a screen of intriguing feminine mystery.'

'Time I what?'

'Never mind. Get your dressing-gown on and get out.'

'But I've got something to tell you! Pietro says that Miss Dryden-Smith was married all the time!'

'Oh, he does? You've left your slippers.'

'Thank you. He says she—oh, Nicholas, open the door! Nicholas! There's lots more to tell you!'

The gush of the taps was the only response, and Julia padded her way to her room, and putting on her pyjamas and dressing-gown, went downstairs to await her brother's arrival at the supper table. But the need to discuss the day's news was too great, and she went to the kitchen to find Pietro.

'Ah, Mees Julia!' Pietro's thick black curls, Roman nose and gleaming white teeth appeared round the door of the larder. 'Mees Julia, to-night is something extra—a special dish!'

There was always, for the Waynes, a special dish.

Pietro Faccini had appeared at Wood Mount a year ago, having met Julia in circumstances which had made him for ever her humble and devoted servant. She had run away from school to fight her sister Lucille's decision to sell the house; he had seen her first, tear-stained, exhausted, dusty and scratched and bleeding, but still full of courage and determination—and he had instantly thrown off the trappings of a brush salesman and put on the apron of a cook in the Wayne household. Nobody had asked him to come; nobody had asked him to stay and cook, but he was here and it looked as though he would be here for ever. And—also self-appointed—her calm solidarity perfectly balancing Pietro's exuberance, was the ex-school Matron, the neat, quiet, formal Miss Cornhill. She was the centre, the hub of the household machine; she listened to Pietro's impassioned pleas for duck and pheasant and melon and sole, and ordered mutton stew with rice. She kept the store cupboard filled with whatever was needed to feed a normal English household, and resisted all Pietro's demands for ingredients with which he could whip up his greatest culinary masterpieces. She kept a cool watch on the household and dealt justly and kindly with the children. Though in charge only of Nicholas's part of the house, she found time to help Roselle and to make small garments for Lucille's expected child. Nicholas considered her quite simply and sincerely as Heaven-sent.

'You have heard, Mees Julia,' asked Pietro, following her into the dining-room, 'about Mees Dryden-Smith?'

'Yes. She nearly changed her Will or something, didn't she?'

'All this time—Ah, your brother is come; now I can bring the special dish! All the time,' went on Pietro, placing it before them and watching them as they ate, 'this Mees Dryden-Smith is married—and nobody don't know nothing about it.' He raised his shoulders to ear-level and spread out his hands and looked, Nicholas thought, more operatic than ever. 'The son—do you know this?—he was to have everything! The spoons, the forks, the pictures, the chairs and the tables—all were to be his. And, of course, the money! And for poor Mees Estelle—nothing! It would have been sad for her, no? But they want to find this man who came to see Mees Dryden-Smith. He is the son, you understand? His arm was in a sling just like Mrs. Ambler's dress—she showed me which one. They want to find him and ask him: Why did you come? Where have you been? Who are you? Perhaps he will hear the news, and he will come—who knows?'

'Nobody,' said Nicholas. 'Julia, your napkin's meant to be used, not looked at.'

'But they don't know——' Pietro took Julia's napkin from its ring, unrolled it and laid it on her lap, '—they don't know where is this son. He come—and phoosh! he vanish! It is like in my village once in Italy—there was a woman and she didn't have a husband and then suddenly, phoosh! Just like this old Mees, she say——'

'You mean she wouldn't have had *anything*, Nicholas?' burst indignantly from Julia.

'Mees Estelle? Nothing,' declared Pietro.

'She's got a profession,' pointed out Nicholas. 'She's got a degree and she would have been able to earn a decent salary teaching.'

'But that house, and all the things in it——'

'It was an ugly house and I don't think she wanted it particularly,' said Nicholas.

'But . . . but will she have to give him a—a share of everything?'

'Give whom?'

'The son. Miss Dryden-Smith's son.'

'No. He isn't entitled to anything at all.'

'If he was going to get all that money, why did he run away?'

'He——' Nicholas stopped hopelessly. It was useless to try to disentangle the threads. Greenhurst would find its own solutions to the mystery surrounding the death of Miss Dryden-Smith. Rumours would grow and multiply and Pietro would hear them when he went into Greenhurst and he would bring them out to Wood Mount and recount them with embellishments. It would be too much to expect Julia to accept the bare facts—and the bare facts were, in any case, difficult to explain.

'I think it was beastly unfair,' she said, 'to want to give the whole lot to him and leave nothing for Miss Dryden.'

'That is just what I think,' said Pietro. 'I—Ah!' He broke off at the sound of a scratching at the door and went to open it. Simon's dog, the huge, shaggy, lumbering Long John came in and, after thrusting a wet nose against Nicholas's hand, went over to Julia and dropped with a sigh at her feet.

'He's all wet—where's he been?' Julia asked Pietro.

'I think that he is in love. He goes away for a long time and when he comes back, he is very tired. There must, I think, be a lady dog,' surmised Pietro. 'When there is a lady dog, all the man dogs race with each other to——'

'Speaking of races,' broke in Nicholas, 'are we going or aren't we?'

'Oh, *can* I go, Nicholas?'

'I don't see why not. I put it to Miss Cornhill, who says races are all right if you don't bet. By which she meant you and not me.'

'But, Nicholas, Pietro says Catalina's going to win—for sure!'

Catalina was the name of Pietro's long-deceased mother. It was also, he had learned quite by chance, the name of a little-fancied horse that was soon to run at a race meeting on a local course. Eager to see the race, he had approached Nicholas with the suggestion that, as the two boys would be home for half-term, they should all go and take a picnic lunch with them. He himself intended to place a modest bet on Catalina, who would romp home well ahead of the rest of the field. With his winnings, he would buy one or two little things he needed: a wireless set, an electric mixer, a new suit of clothes of a superb material that he had fingered in the tailor's shop at Green-hurst, a silk shirt, perhaps two—and a little present for Mees Julia.

'Let us go,' he besought Nicholas earnestly. 'Catalina—you know how much we shall get for our money? If we put on one shilling, we shall get out thirty. If we put two shillings, we shall win sixty. If we——'

'I get it,' said Nicholas. 'Well, it depends whether I can get my car by then.'

'Oh, Nicholas—is it a nice one?' asked Julia, eagerly.

'It will be,' promised Nicholas. 'At the moment its a bit on the shabby side.'

'What colour is it?'

'The little paint that's left on it is a sort of greeny-blue. The engine's running badly but I can fix it sweetly, given time.'

'Did they take your motor bike and sidecar in exchange for the car?'

'In a manner of speaking.'

'How many people will it fit?'

'Two comfortably, two crouched in the back and half a dozen more wedged in here and there.'

'Nicholas . . . do you think Miss Dryden would come with us?' asked Julia. 'There'd be room; Miss Cornhill says she doesn't want to go. Couldn't you ask Miss Dryden? She could sit in front with you and the rest of us could sort of squeeze in behind. It would cheer her up after her aunt dying, and the funeral and everything.'

Estelle was not, however, one of the party bound for the races. Nicholas brought his new purchase to the front of the house and Julia came scrambling down the steps to see it, yelling to her two brothers, now home for a brief half-term holiday. Dominic came rushing out of the house, and then, more soberly, Simon, and at Simon's side as usual came the devoted Long John.

'It isn't as big as I thought,' commented Dominic, walking round the car.

'Can we paint it before we go back to school?' suggested Simon.

'No. She probably looks a bit of a shambles at the moment,' said Nicholas, 'but once I've given her a lick of paint and a new set of tyres and pulled out her engine and put it back in the right places, she'll look like a near approximation to a car. Dominic, go and change those filthy black canvas shoes.'

'They're white canvas shoes,' said Dominic.

'You astound me. Well, go and change them; you're not going to travel in a cramped space with odoriferous footwear. Julia, you can go with him and find out which of your undergarments has gone adrift. Simon, if you're taking Long John you'll need his collar and lead.'

'They're in the car—I've just put them in. Nicholas, can we put some money on Catalina?'

'No. No betting for you young ones.'

'Why not?'

'I'm not absolutely sure,' confessed Nicholas. 'Something to do with the evils of gambling. I can do it because I'm old enough to judge.'

'Judge whether it's right or wrong?'

'No; judge how much I can afford to lose. If Catalina comes home a nose or two ahead of the rest, I dare say you'll come in for a share of the booty. Go and shout at those two and tell them to get a move on, will you?'

They were off. Nicholas and Julia and Dominic in front; at the back, Pietro, Simon and the over-excited Long John, who was seldom privileged to drive in a car and who found the sight of the rapidly-receding house too much for his limited comprehension. They had not gone far when they were halted by the shrill police whistle which Miss Cornhill kept for emergencies like this. Returning, they picked up the picnic baskets which had been left behind, and took in Julia's mackintosh, which she had placed on the car roof and forgotten. Then they were on their way, cramped but cheerful, for a day at the races.

'Well, how's school?' asked Nicholas, as they went.

'All right,' said Dominic. 'You know what? There's a chap in my House who got two teeth knocked out in a hockey match, and they were his second teeth and now he's got false ones and he isn't sleeping in the dorm any more; he's in a room by himself so's he can take them out every night. And the funny part is that he's that chap that I told you about that's got two toes missing. Two toes missing one end and two teeth missing at the——'

'Shut up, you cruel little beast!' shouted Julia.

She seized a fistful of Dominic's hair and he retaliated by grasping her nose and giving it a sharp twist. The battle was brought to an abrupt termination by Nicholas, who stopped the car with a suddenness that threw the combatants against the windscreen.

'Ow! My ear got bumped!' complained Julia.

'One more scene like that,' said Nicholas, 'and I shall open that door and turn you out, both of you, and you can make your own way home. Is that understood?'

'All I did——' began Julia.

'—was behave like the hooligan you are,' finished Nicholas.

'I get all the blame!' she complained, bitterly. 'Just because Dominic——'

'You leave Dominic alone,' requested Nicholas. 'I like him just as he is. There's nothing I like more than having a brother who regales me with amusing stories of his school-mates' infirmities.' He fixed Dominic with a cold eye. 'Do go on,' he invited.

'All I said,' muttered Dominic, scarlet-faced, 'was——'

'There must be some more,' prompted Nicholas. 'Surely that isn't the only one? There must be other poor little devils with something wrong with them? Isn't there anybody with one eye? One leg? No more of the amusing unfortunates struggling under disabilities?'

'No. All right, then—I'm sorry,' said Dominic.

'Look'—Pietro came to the rescue—'In this packet are biscuits that I made—they are very good! Shall we all eat some?'

He unfurled the wrapping and handed them round. Nicholas put the car in motion and addressed Simon over his shoulder.

'It's time you began to exert some authority,' he told him.

'They don't listen to a word I say!' protested Simon.

'Then you must find some way of making them. You're the
eldest, and you can't allow them unlimited rope. I'm a busy
man and I can't keep track of all their criminal activities. I
hereby appoint you my Deputy, and may the Lord help you.
All they need is a mother's tender care and a sharp kick in the
pants twice a day. See to it.'

The course was crowded, and Simon, after losing Long John
twice and finding him again only with the aid of a policeman,
withdrew to the outskirts of the crowd and took his lunch with
him. Nicholas bought a paddock ticket and wandered round
looking at the horses. Dominic decided to watch the race from
the middle of the course and Pietro, having placed his bet on
Catalina, wandered across the grass with Julia until they found
a place from which they could watch the event in comfort. The
day was fine, the course picturesque, the scene gay and colour-
ful. Pietro was enjoying himself to the full, and his commentary halted only when he noticed that Julia was no longer
listening to him but was peering, instead, at an object some
distance away. He followed the direction of her glance, but
could see nothing but a group of more prosperous-looking
race-goers strolling in the direction of the bookmakers' stands.
He heard her speaking in a voice oddly tense.

'Pietro . . .'

'Yes, Mees Julia?'

'Pietro—look over there. No, *there*. Do you see?'

'I don't see nobody we know.'

'But *look*, Pietro'—Julia's voice became insistent—'look
at that man—that man there. Pietro—don't you *see*? The one
with the . . . with his arm in a sling. The sling you told me
about . . . the one that man was wearing when he went to see
Miss Dryden-Smith!

Pietro frowned, his eyes focusing on a tall man who was at
that moment holding a pair of binoculars to his eyes. One arm
was upraised; the other was supported in a sling.

'It's a blue sling,' said Julia, slowly. 'Pietro—oh, Pietro, it's
a—a navy blue sling and it's got sort of little white squiggles

over it and . . . It *must* be, Pietro! It must be him!'

'You think so?' said Pietro, willing to be convinced.

'Of course! Having his arm in a sling wouldn't mean it was him—but *that* sling. . . . Oh, Pietro, it must be!'

'It is a . . .' Pietro clutched at the word coincidence, missed it and used its Italian equivalent. 'It . . . Mees Julia, where are you going?'

'To *ask* him, of course!'

'But——'

'Oh, Pietro, come *on*! Come on, quickly, before he goes back into those places where you have to pay and we can't get in. Come *on*!'

The last words were lost in the breeze; Julia was already hurrying through the crowds. Pietro caught up with her, saw that her face was flushed and her lips set firmly, and uttered no further protest. He knew the signs. Julia was going on a mission.

CHAPTER FIVE

CLIFF HERMANN was enjoying the race meeting very much. He had lost a trifle on the first race, picked it up again on the second, and was now on his way to make his bets for the big race: Catalina. He had got the tip, he felt with satisfaction, straight from the horse's mouth. The secret had been kept, the odds were high. He was in general sceptical about what were known as hot tips, but he believed that Catalina would win, and he meant to back heavily. There was a bookmaker over there giving rather better odds than the rest; now was the time to put the money on.

He took two steps in the direction of the bookmakers' stands and found himself face to face with a little girl. With a murmur of apology, he stepped aside, to find her once more barring his way.

'Oh . . . please . . .' began Julia.

They looked at one another. Julia saw a tall dark man with a face she labelled, with a sinking heart, as a rather cross one. He looked forbidding; he was frowning and he didn't seem . . . approachable. He looked . . . bad-tempered.

Cliff Hermann's temper was an irritable one. He had been the only child of rich parents, and to security had been added success. His manner, normally relaxed, even laconic, changed rapidly when he was confronted with persons or situations he considered obstructing. His irritation once roused, he did not trouble himself to quarrel or even to argue; he merely removed himself to spheres more agreeable. The swift flare of his anger, the abrupt withdrawals were well known in theatrical circles; it was a tribute to his other qualities that his friends remained his friends.

He saw now before him a thin, leggy girl of about eleven or twelve; no beauty, he told himself as he took in the details of her appearance. Hair rusty and rats-tails; face freckled and featureless; clothes undistinguished and dusty and shoes frayed at the toes.

'Excuse me, please, I'd like to pass,' he told her.

'Please—I'd like to talk to you,' said Julia, breathlessly.

'Please,' said a voice behind her.

Cliff looked up. A tall and noble-nosed Latin stood behind the girl and gave the impression of being in attendance—or in league. For an uneasy moment, he wondered whether he were being subjected to an unusual form of begging or soliciting—and then another glance at the girl dismissed the suspicion from his mind. There was an openness, a fearlessness, even an odd sort of dignity about her. Her accent, moreover, was that of a cultured English family. An interesting pair, summed up Cliff—but he had urgent business elsewhere.

'Look,' he began, 'I'm in a hurry. I——'

'Please,' broke in Julia, 'did you go to Greenhurst the other day to see Miss Dryden-Smith?'

'I ... Well, yes; as a matter of fact, I did,' said Cliff. 'So what?'

'She's dead,' said Julia.

'Oh.' For a moment, nonplussed, Cliff felt his way. 'Well, I'm sorry to hear that. But I really didn't know her very well. And now if you'll excuse me, I'll——'

Julia did not stir. This was the man. This was the son who had come out of nowhere and almost robbed Miss Dryden of her inheritance. Here he was. She had found him. They wanted him in Greenhurst; they wanted to ask him why he had run away. If he thought he was going to get away again. . . .

'Please will you wait till I call my brother?' she said, firmly.

'Your ...? Now look.' There was no mistaking the tone; it was that of an angry man. 'If you've anything to say to me, I'll be happy to hear it—later. But right now, I've got some important business to attend to. So if you'll get out of my way, Miss ... whoever you are, I'll be on my way.'

He took two paces to the right. Julia facing him sturdily, took two paces to the left. Both, now, were breathing fast. Cliff's mouth closed in a hard line.

'You there'—he looked directly at Pietro—'will you kindly tell this child——'

'But she's dead and you were there!' cried Julia. 'Don't you see? She's dead! She changed her Will, and she nearly left everything to you—to her son! You're Miss Dryden-Smith's son, but you ran away!'

The words, clear, shrill, arrested the movements of all within hearing. A crowd, interested, but as yet not partisan, closed in round the three ill-assorted figures. Cliff gave a swift glance to left and right and decided that action, and not argument, was called for. He put his hand on Julia's shoulder and pressed her not ungently out of his path.

But the shoulder was unexpectedly thin, the form unexpectedly pliant. Julia stumbled, recovered and was held firm by a suddenly blazing Pietro.

'Ho!' he shouted. 'What you do, eh? You poosh thees lil girl?'

His English deserted him. He broke into swift, fluent and obviously abusive Italian, and Cliff put aside the last remnants of his patience.

'Get her out of my way, will you?' he snapped, and at the sound of his voice, a great sigh like a hiss came from the crowd. American. He was an American. He had come all the way from America to push that little girl. Imagine!

A policeman materialized and made a calm way through the crowd.

'Now then, now then,' he boomed, 'what's going on here?'

'He poosh this little girl,' said Pietro, furiously. 'For nothing, he poosh her—like this.' He illustrated on a hapless bystander whose companion, helping him up, corroborated the evidence.

' 'sright,' he said. 'Pushed her. Saw it with me own eyes.'

'Look, Officer,' began Cliff, desperately, and then stopped. A young man had pushed his way through the crowd and was gazing in dismay at the girl.

'What's going on?' demanded Nicholas of his sister.

Cliff's jaw tightened. Here at last was someone to whom he could speak on equal terms. Whoever the newcomer was, it was clear that he was in authority over this pestilential little girl and her dago attendant.

'I'll tell you what's going on,' he said in a low, furious tone. 'This—this child . . .'

'It's him! Nicholas, don't you see? The sling!' cried Julia.

With a single glance, Nicholas took in the sling and the situation and then spoke calmly to the policeman.

'It's all right, thanks,' he said. 'Sorry you were bothered. This is my sister. I'll straighten it all out.'

The policeman nodded, and departed. The crowd, crestfallen, moved reluctantly away. Over their heads, Cliff saw the starting post, with the restless line of brilliant colour. A pause, a sudden surge, a yell 'They're off' from the spectators, and he knew that his chance of putting money on Catalina was gone. Rage brought the dark colour to his face and he swung furiously round on Nicholas.

'All right—talk,' he said. 'Go on, tell me why I get held up and prevented from making an important bet by a couple of—of——'

'There's no need to take that tone,' said Nicholas, coldly. 'My sister saw you and recognized you as the——'

'So I went to see Miss Dryden-Smith, and she's dead,' broke in Cliff. 'When I left her, she was standing on her two feet. I didn't know her and I'd never seen her before and I presume I'll never see her again, and I'd be glad to know what the hell it's got to do with me.'

'My sister——'

'Your sister called me a bastard, right here in front of fifty people. I've been called one before, but I've usually been able to do something about it. If you——'

'You called on a lady called Miss Dryden-Smith,' Nicholas's calm, icy explanation broke over the other man's furious tones. 'She died of a heart attack shortly after your visit. Immediately you left the house, she began to make out a new Will, leaving everything she had to a son nobody had ever heard of. Nothing but gossip connects you with the affair, but it's felt that something might have taken place at the meeting to explain her action. Her trustees would be glad to be able to put to you one or two questions about the interview you had with her.'

'I had no interview with her. I brought her a parcel of pottery from America at the request of a friend of mine. I gave it to her and she said Thank you and Good-bye. . . . If the information's any use to you, you can use it.'

'Have you any objection to coming to Greenhurst to see Miss Dryden-Smith's lawyer?'

Cliff, for the first time, hesitated. It was clear that his wisest course lay in driving the few miles to Greenhurst, putting the facts of his meeting with Miss Dryden-Smith before the lawyer and so dispersing the rumours that had grown up round his visit. It would not take long—and his afternoon was already ruined. Moreover, if he refused to go, this girl standing here glaring at him, this leech, this limpet ... she had accused him of running away, and she would begin screeching all over again.

He gave Nicholas a cold, level glance of dislike.

'Let's go,' he said.

They turned, Cliff walking between Nicholas and Julia, with Pietro two paces behind—and moved towards one of the gates of the course. As they went, Cliff saw Julia's look of purpose give way gradually to an expression of contentment; glancing over his shoulder, he noted that the Italian's hostility had vanished as swiftly as it had arisen; he had the air of a man going home after a splendid day's sport. Their mission, Cliff saw, was accomplished; they had spied him, brought him down and were taking him home in triumph. The end was accomplished, the means already forgotten. Only Nicholas retained his cold and formal air.

As they neared the exit, Cliff found the escort swerving in order to approach two boys sitting with a large dog near the gates.

'Simon! Dominic!' called Nicholas. 'Come on.'

The boys joined them, and Cliff's eyes went from them to the dog and from the dog to Julia, from Julia to Pietro and then to Nicholas. So ... that's who they were! They were the Waynes. He had by-passed them on his visit to Greenhurst—and now he was trapped in their midst.

He opened his mouth to tell them of his friendship with Robert Debrett, and then closed it again firmly. He would say nothing. He had had more than enough of them all. He was standing here now cooling his heels while the girl, Julia, betting tickets in hand, ran to collect the money that her brother, and her attendant, had won on Catalina. Thirty to one ... here came their winnings—and he had not even been able to place his bet.

Nicholas was speaking to him.

'Have you a car here?'

'I have.'

'Then I think perhaps you'd better follow us; it won't take more than an hour to get back to my place. I'll drop the children and go into Greenhurst with you and put you in touch with Mr. Milward.'

Cliff made no answer. He walked through the lines of waiting vehicles, manoeuvred his sleek car on to the road and watched Nicholas piling the family into the small, shabby, dust-covered one. He watched them as they clambered in, Nicholas at the wheel, with Julia and the younger boy Dominic beside him; the Italian and the older boy and the enormous dog behind. Cliff had an impulse to go over and suggest taking one or more of the passengers into his car, and then decided that if they wanted to split up, they could come and say so. Those who wanted, asked; those who didn't want, didn't ask; those who didn't ask, didn't get.

They moved off, but Nicholas's car, which had run well enough on the outward journey, developed on the homeward stretch a series of faults which brought them, not once, but many times, to a halt. Each time the car in front broke down, Cliff switched off his engine, lit a cigarette and strolled over to watch the row of up-ended posteriors grouped about the defunct engine. Nicholas worked, the engine came to life, they took their places again, and went on to the next check.

Time wore on: one hour, two hours, three. The sun began to go down. They drove, stopped, repaired, drove on and stopped again. At the last-but-one breakdown, Cliff stood next to Simon and found himself addressed in the latter's gentle, polite tones.

'It's a new car,' he explained. 'Nicholas only got it yesterday.'

New car, thought Cliff, was good.

'He's good with engines, but he hasn't had time to—to fix this one yet.'

'I see. Do you. . . .' What did people talk about to young boys? 'Do you often go to the races?'

'No. We only went to-day—Dominic and myself—because we're home for our half-term holiday.'

'And how long is that?'

'Three days. Then we go back for another seven weeks. You're not English, are you?'

'No.'

'Do you like England much?'

'I often come over,' replied Cliff, evasively. 'I have a lot of business to attend to here in England.' How long was this repair going to take?

The repair was done, but when Cliff was about to walk back to his car, he found himself halting to address Simon.

'Would you care to go the rest of the way in my car?'

'Thank you very much. Would you mind if I asked the others if they'd like to come too?'

'I . . . No, not at all; not at all.'

Even the dog, thought Cliff, bitterly, watching them arrange themselves. He got in and drove after the now solitary Nicholas.

'Isn't it wonderful?' said Julia. 'I can stick my legs right out!'

Long John panted his appreciation down Cliff's neck, and Cliff put up a hand to push him away, and then changed his mind. Pushing was out. If he pushed the dog, he'd start another riot. Let the animal go on breathing just wherever he wanted to.

'I think,' Pietro told them, 'I think my brother Giuseppe, in New York, has a car like this. I am not sure but I think so.'

Nicholas's car had stopped again, and he was walking back towards them. He spoke briefly to Cliff.

'She won't go any further,' he said. 'But that gate you see over there is the entrance to our house, Wood Mount. It's too late to look up Mr. Milward, I'm afraid, but there's a good hotel in Greenhurst if you care to go there. The George. But if—he paused and made an obvious effort—'if you'd care to stay with us for the night, we should be happy to have you.'

'Oh—do stay!' urged Julia.

'He's got no pyjamas, idiot,' pointed out Dominic.

'He can have Nicholas's.'

Cliff spoke. The information would have to be given at some time; it had better be given now.

'I know your brother-in-law, Robert Debrett,' he said. 'He and I are old friends.'

Nicholas stared at him for a moment in astonishment, and then his manner became one of calm decision.

'Then there's no question of The George,' he said. 'Will you drive on up to the house? I'll join you in a moment.'

Cliff drove on. The car turned into the big gateway and halted at the foot of the long flight of steps leading up to the front door. The passengers scrambled out, the dog barked. Pietro hurried inside with the empty picnic baskets and Julia and Dominic had their usual race up the steps. Simon looked up at Cliff.

'Do come in,' he invited.

CHAPTER SIX

NICHOLAS caught Cliff up at the top of the flight of steps and led him into the house. He dismissed the children, took Cliff into the drawing-room and, with a word of excuse, withdrew. A middle-aged woman then appeared, introduced herself as the housekeeper, Miss Cornhill, and led Cliff to a bedroom on the ground floor. She showed him the bathroom, assured him of a ready supply of hot water, and left him. Next there was a thump on the door and Dominic appeared, holding a pair of pyjamas and a dressing-gown.

'You haven't got your own night things with you, have you?' he enquired, wriggling on to the bed and regarding the visitor with calm grey eyes.

'No. I didn't know I was going to be away for a night.'

'You were angry with Julia, weren't you, a bit?'

'I was—well, yes, I was mad at first, because she stopped me when I was going to put some money on Catalina.'

Dominic nodded understandingly, and Cliff looked at him. This was the one Robert had called beautiful—and over there in New York, the adjective, applied to a ten-year-old boy, had sounded, to say the least, overdone—but here, with the boy before him, Cliff found that it was not easy to find another word that would describe him so well. He had not yet met all the members of the family, but Roselle's skin could be no fairer, Lucille's eyes no finer. He was as beautiful, this boy, as his sister Julia was plain; it was difficult to think of them as brother and sister.

'What part of America do you come from?' asked Dominic.

'New York.'

'Oh. We're not doing that bit at school. We're doing Chile and Peru and that.'

'That's South America,'

'When are you going back?'

'Very soon.'

'Will you see Robert?'

'I hope so. He'll want to hear all about you all.'

'I s'pose he's heard Lucille's going to have a baby?'

'Naturally. If the father doesn't know, who would?'

'It didn't really begin until after he'd gone—not to notice,' said Dominic carelessly, and stood up. 'If I were you, I'd get into the bathroom before Julia does. She takes all the hot water and stays in for ages.'

'Well, thanks for telling me.'

Some time later, Cliff left his bedroom, hesitated in the hall and then opened a door to find himself in a large drawing-room. At the far end, standing by a window, was a woman he had no trouble in identifying. He went across the room with long strides and took her hands in his own, looking down at her with a smile that transformed his face and did more than anything else to explain why he kept his friends.

'You're Lucille and I'm glad to know you,' he said. 'And . . . congratulations,' he added gently. 'Robert told me all about him. He's to be called Nicholas Daniel. Right?'

'Quite right.' Lucille laughed and Cliff, taking in her loveliness, understood for the first time why Robert Debrett, so well-armoured and for so long against women's wiles, had fallen victim at last to an unknown girl in a quiet country town.

He heard her low rich voice.

'Congratulations in a week or two,' she said. 'At the moment, just condolences! I'm at the bored stage. Tell me about Robert, please.'

Cliff shook his head with every appearance of regret.

'He's not the guy he was. Time was when he was a man among men; we used to meet and carouse and wine and . . . and so on, and wherever we went, there was Robert Debrett, right in the middle. But now he's quiet and aloof and there's a questing look in his eye. And now that I've seen you, I don't wonder at it any more. You know something? He's a lucky guy.'

'And he asked you to come and see us—but you must have decided not to, because it was you, wasn't it, who——'

'Oh my, oh my,' groaned Cliff, 'here it comes.'

'Well, sit down and tell me why we frightened you off,' said Lucille. 'The cigarettes are in that box—no, the lighter doesn't light; you'll have to use your own. You know, of course, that you've got yourself thoroughly mixed up with our local mystery?'

'Yes, I know. The Last Hours of Miss Dryden-Smith. I don't know anything about it yet—except what your sister . . .' he paused and groaned once more. 'Julia!' he said, in a tone of despair. 'How was I to know. . . . Tell me, is she a child who retains her first impressions of anybody? Because if so, I'm——'

'Julia won't hold anything against you, but Pietro might,' said Lucille.

'Yes. I poosha da lil girl,' said Cliff. 'But I seem to have lived it down. As a matter of fact, all I did was put a hand on her shoulder and—and sort of urge her. But darn it, Lucille, there I was, on my way to make a pile of dough, and who cared? They'd got their bets placed—why should they worry if I lost a few thousand dollars? And if they told you I got mad, then they're right; I did. And I'm sorry that I did, because, for Robert's sake as well as my own, I would have liked to get on the right side of this family. Your brother Nicholas——'

'Why didn't you help him when his car broke down?'

'I told you—I was mad, and when I get off the beam, I stay off for a little while. And now I'm sorry. But Julia yelled out loud in front of a crowd of strangers that I was the son of Miss Dryden-Smith. That shakes a man.'

'I suppose it does. But there was something behind Julia's persistence. Miss Dryden-Smith's niece, whose name is Estelle Dryden, taught for a time at Julia's school in Greenhurst. She taught Literature, and she's the only person in Julia's school history who has ever succeeded in getting any work, or even an interest, out of my sister. We're all very grateful to her, but Julia isn't just grateful—she's just adoring. She'd heard a garbled story of your visit to Miss Dryden-Smith, and she got the idea that you were needed in some way to clear up the mystery for Estelle Dryden. When Julia gets an idea, she hangs on to it—but I'm glad she brought you back to Wood Mount. Do you know anything about this son?'

'Not a thing. Not a single thing. A friend of mine in New York came to me and said he knew an old lady in this place Greenhurst, and from time to time he sent her parcels of china—I take it china was one of her hobbies. I brought over this Mexican stuff and she didn't even open it and I don't think I was in the room more than twenty minutes. The whole thing was nothing to do with any son or any new Will. I simply happened along at that time, that's all. I drove away without coming out here to see you because I meant to come another——'

'—some other time.' Lucille laughed. 'Poor Cliff! Well, in the morning, Nicholas will take you in to see Mr. Milward, and you can tell him to cross you off his list of suspects.'

'Milward . . . he'll be the father of Jeff, who's the husband of your sister Roselle—correct?'

'Quite correct. I hope Robert didn't bore you with too many details? Oh, here's Nicholas.'

'Dinner's on the table—shall we go in?' asked Nicholas, and at the formality of his tone, Cliff turned appealingly to Lucille.

'You hear that?' he said. 'He sounds sort of cold and un-friendly. I don't blame him—but tell him I said I was sorry. Tell him I lost a lot of money on Catalina. Tell him I've got a mean temper. Tell him that the real reason I didn't give him a hand with his carburettor was because I wouldn't know a carburettor if someone showed me one. I haven't seen the inside of a car's works since I was fifteen; I buy a car and I drive it and then I turn it in for a new one before it begins to need any nursing. Tell him I didn't mean to push his little sister. And tell him that his disposition doesn't look to me any sweeter than my own. If my temper's tricky, his goes on work-ing for longer. Tell him, if he'll forget, I'll forgive—or you can switch those around. Tell him he's my host, and shouldn't show his feelings. Go on; go ahead; tell him.'

He faced Nicholas and held out a hand.

'Hi,' he said, 'or do we rub noses?'

Nicholas grinned.

'We go to dinner,' he said. 'And having introduced the world bastard into this family, you can occupy yourself in tell-ing them all exactly what it means. Let's go.'

*   *   *

In the morning, Cliff rose, dressed and made his way to the dining-room. There was nobody there and all the plates but one had been cleared, but on a sideboard he found fruit and cereals, and was helping himself to both when Pietro's head appeared round the door.

'Oh . . . good morning,' said Cliff.

'Good morning.' Pietro's voice was warm with friendliness; yesterday might never have been. 'You like tea? Coffee? Toast? Eggs fried wiss bacon? Eggs fried wiss tomato? Eggs boiled three minutes, four minutes? Omelette wiss herbs, wissout herbs? Omelette wis mushroom, wissout mushroom? Omelette——'

'I guess I'll just have coffee and two fried eggs,' said Cliff. 'Oh—and toast.'

He strolled into the kitchen to watch Pietro as he cooked, and listened to his lively flow of conversation. He watched the tall figure bending over the frying-pan and felt that it was in some way incomplete; an anachronism. Those thick black curls, that nose, the flamboyant gestures—all these called for a setting that was now out of date. He ought to be turning a barrel organ or pushing one of those old ice-cream carts with a gay striped canopy over it.

'You live in New York, no?' he asked Cliff.

'Yes.'

'I, too, live there one day. I will save the fare and go. My brother, Giuseppe, he sent me the fare, but it went—phoosh! Like that. One day I shall go—when Mees Julia is married, perhaps. But I should not like to go now, because who will cook here? There is only me. There is a Mees who is the housekeeper, but she don' cook—and she don' let me cook the things I want to. She doesn't understand good cooking; she knows what I could do if she would buy me all the things I need—but she will not buy them. No fancies, she says all the time. No richness. No fats. No gateaux, no flambeaux, no—no nothing. Only the English cooking, she says. She will buy nothing, nothing but only what you see in this cupboard—see?

It is terrible! But with that, I do how I can.' Pietro, in one fluid movement, produced a warmed plate, turned the eggs on to it, picked up the coffee-pot, extracted the toast and led Cliff to the dining-room.

'There! Now you will eat—but if you had tried my omelette duchesse . . . perhaps if you are still hungry when you have——'

'No. No, thanks. This is fine.'

'After, you will go out to play with the children, yes? The boys, they will not be here for long; this is a little holidays for them, and in two days they will go to school again. But Mees Julia will not go back for one week—her school is at Green-hurst and her holidays is longer. She is in the garden. Simon is not there—I think he is looking for Long John—that's his dog—you know? You saw him before.'

Cliff nodded. He was not greatly interested in the family news items. He had little experience of children, young or not so young; his brief encounters with them had left with him a feeling that he was more at home in adult society. He would avoid the younger Waynes as much as possible; certainly he had no intention of becoming involved in their juvenile world.

Miss Cornhill came in, wished Cliff a calm good morning and led Pietro away for a discussion of the day's menus. Cliff finished his breakfast, poured the last drops of excellent coffee from the pot and sat listening to sounds which, coming from the garden, gave him a fairly accurate idea of what the various members of the family were doing. Dominic seemed to be up a tree some distance away; Julia, at ground level, was shouting directions as he let down a rope. Nicholas, to judge from the occasional splutter of an engine, was in the garage working on his car.

Cliff rose, strolled into the drawing-room and was about to leave it by the long window leading on to the lawn, when the sound of the door opening behind him made him turn. A girl came in, stood still for a moment to look at him and then came hurrying across the room towards him.

'You must be the one,' she said.

He looked at her and liked what he saw. His first thought, that she might be Roselle, whom he had not yet met, vanished as he studied her features. This girl was not blue-eyed, and would not have been labelled pretty—but she was a good deal more than pretty, Cliff decided. She was . . . perhaps piquante would do for now. He liked her eyes, long and narrow and alive with intelligence, and her soft curved mouth.

'I'm the one,' he said, 'and which one are you?'

'I'm Estelle Dryden,' she said, and rendered Cliff Hermann, for the first time in his life, speechless.

Estelle Dryden! She was the niece. She was the Miss Dryden of whom he had been told and who he had imagined, without cause or sense, to be a somewhat younger version of the aunt: spare, dry, caustic. This was the school-teacher. This was the Miss Dryden who had come into her inheritance on the afternoon he had visited her aunt.

The fragments of the story which he had heard, so far, without any great interest, fell suddenly into place and gave him the first clear picture of the events of that sunny afternoon on which he had first come to Greenhurst. He saw himself going into the big house, parcel under arm. He saw his expression, which he had not troubled to make agreeable—and Miss Dryden-Smith's, which she had not exerted herself to make welcoming. He had come—and gone. Miss Dryden-Smith had begun to alter her Will—and died. For the first time he saw clearly how he had come to be linked so closely with the events of that day. Nobody had any idea who he was; they had known only that, on his departure, Miss Dryden-Smith had sat down to reveal a secret that had, up to that time, been hidden even from those who knew her best. And if death had not arrested her hand, this girl standing before him would have been disinherited.

'Well . . . and so you're Miss Dryden,' he said blankly, at last.

'You sound surprised. Did you expect me to be younger or older?'

'Much, much older. It was stupid of me, but nobody . . . Lucille said you were Julia's school-teacher——'

'I am; at least, I was for half a term, while one of the mistresses was ill. But apart from that, Wood Mount has always been a second home to me. I've known the Waynes almost all my life, and Lucille and I are great friends.'

She sat on a low chair and motioned him to one opposite.

'Nicholas rang up this morning and said he was going to bring you in to see Mr. Milward as soon as he'd got his car going.'

'He could have used mine.'

'If yours is that sleek monster standing outside, I can see why using his own would be more or less a matter of principle,' she told him with a boyish grin. 'But I couldn't wait for you to come out—and so I came here. Nicholas told me about Julia finding you at the races yesterday. I gather that you were . . . there's a word you use for what they did to you.'

'Corralled?'

'That'll do. You're the playwright, aren't you?'

'That's a flattering way of putting it. I'm a playwright, yes.'

'Is Robert going to be in your new play?'

'I hope so.'

'I wish I could have seen you pushing Julia.'

'Oh—wait now—I——'

'—pushed Julia. Have you had breakfast?'

'I have,' he answered.

'And you feel well?'

'I feel very well.'

'I'm surprised,' she said. 'If you pushed Julia, it's more than likely Pietro put something in your breakfast that'll curl you up before long.'

'Pietro and I are good friends.'

'Nonsense. Pietro is Julia's bodyguard, and you pushed Julia.'

'I pushed her once and only once,' he pointed out, goaded.

She laughed and then spoke soberly.

'I've got hundreds of questions to ask you. You'll have to answer them all again when you meet the Trustees, but I couldn't wait. May I ask you—oh—a lot of things!'

'Go ahead. But first,' he said, 'let me say this: I have not and never had any connection with your aunt, Miss Dryden-Smith. I never in my life saw her before I went to her house. I never heard of her until someone in New York heard me say that I was coming to England and asked me if I'd bring over a parcel for an old lady who collected china and pottery. I am not, in case you or anybody else happens to suspect it, Miss Dryden-Smith's son. I have—that is, I had until she died—a perfectly adequate mother of my own. I wasn't adopted and I wasn't left on anybody's doorstep. My father and my mother were married in Massachusetts and I was born in New York a year after the marriage, so that I can not only claim to be somebody else's son, but I can state that I'm perfectly legitimate. I can produce, if necessary, friends and relations a-plenty to prove that they were in the next room while the happy event was taking place, and that I'm a Hermann and nothing but a Hermann. Now go ahead with those questions.'

'Nobody—except the sensation-mongers—ever went so far as to think that you were my aunt's son. It would have been too . . . too theatrical. But what we feel—that is, what old Mr. Wylie and Uncle Bill Milward and I feel—is that there must be some connection between your visit and her actions immediately after it. Something must have happened while you were with her to—to make her do what she did, or what she so nearly did. I had lunch with her an hour or two before your visit and I know that she was well, and normal, and completely herself. Less than three hours later, she's writing a new Will, knowing it to be her last. Something must have happened while you were there—something must have been said. . . .'

'Nothing happened and nothing was said,' declared Cliff. 'I

went in; I guess I looked kind of sour, because the day had
turned out better than it had looked when I telephoned your
aunt, and I felt the whole visit was a waste of time—if you'll
forgive me.'

'Go on.'

'She was in the drawing-room; the old man who let me in
took me to the door, opened it and left me. Your aunt asked
me to sit down, and I did. We said this and that about the
weather and I got up to give her the parcel. She didn't open
it.'

'She never did open it. It was found, when she died, just as
you'd brought it.'

'So it couldn't have been anything to do with the parcel.
Well, she asked me what I was doing, and I told her.'

'Told her what exactly?'

'I said I was over here to talk about a play of mine that's
being put on in London in the autumn. She didn't seem interested. She said—as far as I can remember—that she didn't
go for drama—only music.'

'That's quite right.'

'So then I think things kind of petered out. She said, I
think, how did I come down, and I said by car—and that
surprised her a little, because she looked at my arm in the
sling, and seemed to think it was out of action. I said no, it
wasn't entirely out of action; I rested it now and then, but I
could use it. She said how did I hurt it and I told her and then
she——'

'What did you tell her?'

'I said that I'd flown over—I think maybe I made a sort of
joke about flying the Atlantic safely and getting injured on the
tarmac. A coach that was taking a bunch of us to the airport
buildings hit another coach that was taking some passengers
out to their plane. Nothing really happened—I don't think
either of the coaches was travelling over thirty, but the one I
was in got the worst of it. Some of us were hurt and taken to
hospital and then most of us were patched up and allowed to

leave. I don't know what interest all that would have for your aunt, unless the hospital was the one where she had the baby—or something. But that was the whole of the meeting between us. She said she was sorry she couldn't ask me to stay, because she was feeling tired.'

'*Was* she feeling tired?'

'I . . . well, at first I thought it was a sort of excuse to get rid of me—but then I looked at her and she did seem to me to be looking . . . kind of pale, I think.'

'Ill, you mean?'

'I . . . I honestly don't know, Miss Dryden. Yes. Yes, I think she did look ill, because I asked her if I could call somebody to help her, but she said no. She was standing by the window—the light was behind her.'

'But . . . but it wasn't at all like her to say she was feeling tired. She'd never have admitted it.'

'She explained that her heart wasn't strong.'

'She *said* that?'

'Yes.'

'I don't understand,' Estelle stared at him, her eyes blank with speculation. 'I can't understand why she'd say a thing like that.'

'But she did have a bad heart?'

'Oh—yes. But nobody ever heard her admit it. If she felt ill—and she often did—she'd go to any lengths to make us believe that she was all right.'

'It could have been an excuse. She wanted me to go, and that was perhaps the only way she could get rid of a stranger without seeming to be impolite.'

'Seeming to be impolite never worried my aunt. But you said you did think she looked ill?'

'Yes. I remember that I waited out by my car for a moment or two, wondering if I ought to go back and see if she was all right. Then I saw somebody who looked like a housekeeper or a companion going in by the side door, and I went away.'

'That was the housekeeper, Mrs. Ambler. She heard your

car drive away and went straight into the drawing-room—and a few minutes later, my aunt was dead. And so now you see why I think there must have been some connection between your visit and her death?'

'Yes, I see. Unless . . .'

'Well?'

'You said her heart wasn't strong. If the attack began to come on when I was with her, she might have felt that it was a really bad one, and she might have decided to put into operation a plan she'd had for some time. I don't know anything about this; I'm just guessing—but if she did have a son, and if she had altered the Will in the ordinary course of her lifetime, she would have had a lot of explaining to do. Suppose she told herself that she would keep the son dark—until the very end? Does that sound at all probable to you?'

'No.' Estelle shook her head. 'No, it doesn't. Some of her attacks were all but fatal—she'd never leave an important thing like a change of Will to the chance of being able to write it just before she died. No—it wasn't that, Mr. Hermann. Something—*something* happened while you were there.'

'The name's Cliff, and I'd be glad if you would use it. There is one thing,' he went on slowly, 'that seems a possibility to me. But I suppose that it's occurred to all of you here, too.'

'You mean that she did have a son, and that in some way you reminded her of him?'

'Yes. But that doesn't hold water either, because if I was like her son, wouldn't she have shown it when she first laid eyes on me?'

'Not necessarily. Perhaps that's why she was so abrupt when she met you. Perhaps she was . . . was holding her emotions in check and in the end the effort exhausted her and she had to ask you to go.'

He smiled at her.

'Maybe you could write plays, too,' he suggested.

'You think that's too wild a theory?'

'I guess no theory's likely to get you very far. There aren't many clues to get hold of. And as things are, it doesn't matter very much, does it, if you never find him at all?'

She hesitated.

'How would you feel,' she asked, 'if you inherited something that should, in justice, have gone to somebody else?'

'I'd thank my stars and hang on tight.'

'Well, that would be very high-principled of you, but——'

'You mean that you want to hand over this inheritance—on principle?'

'Well, you can laugh, but it's partly true. I'm quite sure that my aunt did have a son, and that at the end, she felt that she wanted him to have—everything. I'd like to find him. I don't want to sound foolishly sentimental, but I'd like to find him and let him know that his mother thought of him at the end. I'd like to know whether he knew who he was—knew he was her son.' She frowned. 'Being left in the dark—in the air like this, coming into money simply because someone died before they could . . . make other arrangements . . .'

'If there is a son, haven't you any idea where or when or even why she had one?'

'None—and I don't suppose we'll ever find out. When she was young, when her heart was strong and didn't trouble her, she was a great traveller. She used to go away and stay away for long periods. She travelled too far, and too often to make it possible for us to—to——'

'Follow a trail?'

'Yes.'

'You could advertise for him.'

'How could I?' She spread out her hands helplessly. 'What do I call him? I can't insert notices in reputable newspapers asking for the son of Miss Dryden-Smith to——'

'—to show up. No, I suppose not. And if you did, you'd have a trail of hopefuls making their way to Greenhurst and putting forward phoney claims.'

'So you see? Nicholas said that—oh, here he is! Nicholas,' she went on without a pause, 'Mr. Hermann has told me every- thing that happened at that meeting with Aunt Mary . . . and . . . *nothing*!'

Nicholas smiled at her. He was wearing a pair of working overalls and he had not come into the room; he was at the door, leaning carelessly against it. Something in the quiet glance that rested on Estelle stirred speculation in Cliff, and following upon speculation came certainty.

So young Julia, he mused, was not the only one whose heart was given into those small brown hands. Julia—and this Adonis standing there giving off petrol fumes. He loved her— and she had inherited her aunt's fortune, which must be con- siderable—and all he owned was the ground floor of a house and a contraption on four wheels that went by the name of car. And an up-and-coming business in that little town. She was in his house, and her easy familiarity in it made it clear that she spent as much time in it as in her own. Girl and boy. . . . They had grown up together, and it was easy to read the feelings of one of them.

And the other?

Cliff was not sure. She looked, in her low chair, relaxed and at ease. She put out a hand and Nicholas came forward and pulled her to her feet; she stood beside him, her head on a level with his shoulder, her hand still carelessly in his. Some- thing about her—her simplicity, her effortless charm, her absurd nose, her curving mouth—added up to an attraction that Cliff had never felt in any other woman. He wanted her to go on talking . . . to him. He wanted to stay in this drawing- room with the sun streaming in through the great windows on to light gold hair. He wished it were possible, as it was pos- sible at a rehearsal of one of his plays, to go back to the moment of her entrance and run through the scene again . . . and again. But then there would always be the entrance of Nicholas. . . .

Nicholas.

He remembered the words he had spoken in this room the evening before, and his lips curved in a mirthless smile.

Perhaps, after all, he told himself grimly, there would be no rubbing of noses.

CHAPTER SEVEN

THERE was nothing, reflected Cliff two hours later, like work. Work was a fine thing. Everybody should work. Everybody should have some kind of office to which, day by day, they had to go, an office which claimed them from morning to evening and prevented them from staying at home and monopolizing the attention of girls like Estelle Dryden.

He had seen Nicholas driving away in his patched-up car; he hoped very much that the Greenhurst Travel Agency would flourish, and Nicholas with it—but he found it reassuring to know that, while the younger man had to be in Greenhurst making arrangements for Hellenic cruises or seaside holidays for his clients, he himself was free to sit on this pleasant lawn at Wood Mount discussing with Estelle Dryden the endless puzzles and probabilities raised by her aunt's Will. He could spend long hours with her, watching the play of expression on her lovely yes, it was a lovely face. He could listen to her quick, light, eager voice and her gurgling laugh. From time to time he could make lazy suggestions.

'You could draw up a time sheet,' he said to her. 'You could do a survey of where she went, and when, and from it you could make a rough guess at where or when she had this son.'

'But it would take ... oh—ages!' Estelle made a hopeless gesture, and the hammock on which she was sitting wobbled dangerously. 'We wouldn't, in any case, know where to begin.'

'Oh, yes, you would.' Cliff leaned back in his battered but

comfortable wicker chair and lit another cigarette. 'Oh, yes, you would. For one thing, her Bank would tell you quite a lot; she must have drawn travellers' cheques for her journeys. She must have notified her staff when she was going, and where.'

'She probably did, but I can't go about digging up ex-butlers and ex-maids and questioning them. I should simply go round in circles and end up just where I'd begun.'

'It might be interesting.'

'We're not all people of leisure, like you,' pointed out Estelle. 'We——'

'I work as hard as anyone—when I work.'

'That ought to be your epitaph—in the past tense, of course. "He worked as hard as anyone—when he worked." But in between these gruelling sessions, Mr. Hermann, you have plenty of time to delve into the past of old ladies who were thought to be completely conventional and who turned out to be nothing of the kind. Aunt Mary . . . and a love affair,' she said, dreamily. 'It doesn't go, somehow.'

'Why not? She wasn't always middle-aged and sharp-tongued.'

'Now that's where you're wrong. I think she was. Uncle Bill says she was a handsome girl and so she may have been—but she told me herself that she couldn't remember anybody in her life she'd really got on well with. She found most people irritating. She didn't get on with anybody in Greenhurst—except me. I think she was fond of me in her own way.'

'But all the same, you believe that she fell in love and had a child?'

'Had a child, yes; fell in love . . . it doesn't sound like Aunt Mary.'

'Then what? You feel that she was trekking across the Sahara and a bold bad sheik galloped up, seized her and ravished her?'

'Never. She would have peered at him with narrowed eyes and analysed his horrid motives in short, caustic phrases and made him see the incident in an entirely unsentimental light.

Horse sense—that was her war cry. She would have applied horse sense to the sheik and his lusty ambitions, and he would have galloped off and left her where he found her—unharmed.'

He looked at her and smiled, and she wondered if he knew how well he smiled, and decided that he did. He was a man, she thought, who would study effects. He was keenly intelligent, and so he must be well aware that his lean dark good looks might be used—if he wished—to almost devastating effect. She wondered, as her aunt had wondered, whether his habitually forbidding expression was natural or a mask worn to disguise gentler qualities—or to deter intrusive strangers.

'Robert asked you to come here, didn't he?' she asked.

'He did.'

'But you didn't come, although you came down to Greenhurst to call on my aunt. Why didn't you drive out to Wood Mount that day?'

'I . . . well, it seems silly now,' he confessed, 'but I wanted to get back to London. I drove back by way of Wood Mount and took a look at the house, but I remembered that Lucille was on the point of having a baby, and I remembered that there were young children in the house and I'm no hand with children, and so . . . I drove on. And now I'm sorry.'

'Why?'

'Well, for one thing,' he said, slowly. 'because Lucille is lovelier than I could have believed possible and meeting her wasn't the embarrassment I thought it would be.'

'Embarrassment?'

'A woman doesn't as a rule like to be confronted by strangers when she's a week or two off producing a baby.'

'Well, I wouldn't know about that,' said Estelle, judiciously. 'Proceed.'

'I like the children. I didn't think that I would, but I do. I don't say I'd be any hand at making friends with them, but I like the look of them. I like that Julia and that future threat to women's hearts, Dominic. I like Simon and his serious look. I even like that theatrical Italian guy, and he seems to like me.'

'Even though you pushed Julia.'

'Look—you said that. You said that twice.'

'I'm just seeing that you keep it in mind. You look to me like a man who puts his mistakes behind him with ease and without regret—or remorse.'

'All right. So I'm an unprincipled son of a——'

'Don't finish that,' warned Estelle. 'You've used one strong word here already. When are you going back to America?'

He hesitated and then, to his own astonishment, heard himself speaking in undecided tones.

'I don't know. I . . . I've a lot of business to see to yet.'

'Where do you live?' she asked, with frank curiosity. 'I mean, where's your home?'

'New York. Where else?'

'I can think of a lot of nicer places.'

'You can? Name them.'

'Oh . . . older places; quieter places.'

'You know New York?'

'No.'

'Then how can you make comparisons? Don't you want to see it?'

'Not much. At least,' she amended, 'it's on my, so to speak, travel list, but there are so many other places I want to see more.'

'As for example?'

'Oh . . .'

'Rome, Venice, Istanbul?'

'No. Not the highlights. You see so many pictures, you read so many accounts of them, that you can get a fair idea without spending your money on actually going there yourself. No. . . . I'd like to see places that aren't splashed on travel posters all over the world. Small places; little-known places.'

'Specify.'

'Oh . . . as one example, that convent in Spain called Las Huelgas, where you can see the actual clothes that Alfonso VIII and Eleanor of England wore in their coffins—her red and

blue and gold headdress and the cushion . . . and the tunic that
was on Ferdinand de la Cerda. The things they were actually
buried in. . . .'

'Sounds like fun,' he commented. 'When are you setting
off?'

'Some time. I want to see little, unheard-of villages in
France and Spain. I want to find places for myself, and settle
in them for a time instead of rushing through them. I'd like to
talk to old Italian peasants near my little whitewashed villa,
and get to know them a little. Wouldn't you?'

'If I could do it all in comfort—yes.'

She looked at him curiously.

'What have you seen?'

'New York, London, Paris, Rome, Madrid, Lisbon,
Madrid, Rome, Paris, London, New York.'

'You collect capitals?'

'I feel at home in them. I know a lot of people in them. I do
business in them. I know the best hotels, the best restaurants,
the tucked-away surprises.'

'And, of course, the airports.'

'And the airports. You think I've missed something?'

'How do I know?' she asked. 'I suppose I've missed a lot
more. You lead a sort of international life, and I've been here
in Greenhurst most of my life. Aunt Mary didn't encourage
travel. I used to wonder why, since she'd done so much of it
herself, but——'

'—but now you see that she might have had her reasons.'

'Yes. But I think that if I'd had your—your opportunities, I
would have strayed out of the cities more than you appear to
have done.' She added a gentle sentence. 'I'm not criticizing
you.'

'Yes, you are,' said Cliff. 'But go ahead; I like listening to
you.'

'We're not getting very far with the mystery of Aunt Mary's
son, are we?'

Cliff pulled himself up just short of telling her that he had

lost the fleeting interest he had had in her Aunt Mary and her
Aunt Mary's son. The aunt was dead; the niece was alive, de-
liciously, enticingly alive. He could not remember when he
had felt so much pleasure in talking to a girl. His tastes ran to
older and more experienced women. He moved in circles in
which most of the women were beautiful, and beneath their
surface softness hard and grim careerists. They had looks and
brains, and the ability to use both to the best advantage. This
girl had looks and brains—and there the resemblance ended.
She had a freshness and charm that were all but irresistible. He
was sitting here—he, Cliff Hermann—listening to a small-
town school-teacher. And liking it. He did not analyse the feeling; he noted it and decided that he would spend as much time
as possible in her company while he remained at Wood Mount
—and he meant to remain at Wood Mount until his return to
America. Lucille would ask him to stay on, and he would
accept the offer; he would go up to London and fetch his
luggage and spend a pleasant interlude in this green retreat.

Estelle got to her feet, and Cliff hauled himself reluctantly
out of his chair.

'Where are you going?' he asked.

'Home. Back to Greenhurst—when I've been up to see
Lucille and Roselle.'

'Why can't you stay to lunch?'

She threw back her head and laughed—a long, gurgling
laugh of pure amusement.

'What's so funny?' he asked, unsmiling.

'You.' She sobered. 'Or perhaps it isn't amusing. What
makes you think you can issue invitations to lunch?'

'You're an old friend of the family—aren't you?'

'Certainly—but you're not.'

'Give me time. Look'—he spoke with unwonted impulsive-
ness—'don't go.'

'I have to go. I want to talk to Lucille, and to Roselle—and
they want to talk to me. They want to hear more about this
Will. All this may seem to you like a—a storm in a teacup—

coffee-cup—but to us it's . . . it's exciting. You only saw my aunt for twenty minutes; the Waynes knew her for twenty years. They . . . Oh, hello, Julia.'

'Hello, Miss Dryden.' Julia's face was pink, but she was showing no other sign of emotion. 'I brought you these.'

She held out a little bunch of flowers, newly gathered, but already looking rather the worse for having been squeezed in Julia's tense fist.

'Thank you, Julia. They're lovely! Will you put them in water for me, please, and I'll take them with me when I go.'

'Yes, I will.' Julia took them and gave Cliff a friendly glance. 'Good morning, Mr. Hermann.'

'Good morning, Julia,' answered Cliff. 'Spent your winnings yet?'

'No. I didn't bet. Nicholas wouldn't let me.'

She streaked away and the two stood looking after her.

'Adorer?' said Cliff.

'Thank goodness, yes,' said Estelle, feelingly. 'It's making her study—actually study. Study and Julia . . . that used to be a contradiction in terms, but now she's working, and if she's doing it for love of me instead of for the love of learning, what does it matter?'

They strolled slowly towards the house, and Cliff studied it through half-closed eyes.

'It's a lovely place.'

'Yes,' she agreed, 'it's lovely.'

'It was up for sale. Did Robert buy it?'

'No. Robert and Jeff and Nicholas bought one third each. Robert and Lucille aren't here much; they use the top floor as a sort of country cottage. Roselle and Jeff live on the middle floor and Nicholas is the head of the family on the ground floor.'

'Sounds kind of cramped.'

She gave him a swift upward glance in which he saw more than a hint of coldness.

'It isn't at all cramped. Some families can be close together and still get on well and not feel crowded.'

'I'll take your word for it. I never had a family.'

She frowned up at him.

'Haven't you a wife?' She made it sound as though he ought to have.

He answered without thinking.

'I was engaged once,' he said. 'She was seventeen; I was twenty—almost. It lasted a year—almost.' He came to a sudden halt, causing her to stop, and looked down at her with amazement spreading slowly over his face. 'You know something?' he said, wonderingly. 'I . . . I haven't told that to anybody in years. And never to a stranger. I—I don't know what made me.'

'It's all right.' Her tone was placid. 'It's just the schoolmistress in me, that's all. People think that teachers are giving out all the time, but they're not; they're trained to draw out, too. If they didn't have the qualities of inspiring trust, how could they ever hope to be successful with children? Why didn't you stay engaged?'

'Because we didn't stay in love. One day—and I mean one day, just suddenly, like that—we looked at each other and whatever had been there was gone. The engagement couldn't end fast enough for either of us. It was good enough while it lasted. And it acted as a sort of inoculation; that was more than fifteen years ago and I haven't had the bug in my system since.'

She made no reply. She was looking at a point far above his head, and Cliff, turning and following the direction of her glance, saw high up on a great oak tree the outline of a sturdy little wooden building.

'Dominic's tree house?' he asked.

'Yes. It terrifies me to watch him up there. Nicholas has just helped him to fix up lights in it.'

Nicholas. He appeared, Cliff noted, with monotonous regularity in the conversation. A man could get tired of hearing the name of another man dropped too frequently into his ears. He would have liked to find some way of telling this girl that other women to whom he showed the frank partiality he was showing her would have returned the compliment by giving him their undivided attention. It was at least tactful.

But there was no opportunity now to say anything more to Estelle. She told him she was going upstairs to see Lucille and Roselle; a moment later, he found himself alone.

He turned and walked slowly back to his chair, dismayed at the annoyance that flooded him. Then surprise drove out other emotions, for on the hammock vacated by Estelle sat Julia, swinging slowly to and fro.

'Did Simon have breakfast with you?' she asked.

'No. Why?'

'Because then he must have had it before Dominic and me. I think he's looking for Long John.'

'Long . . . oh, that's his dog?'

'Yes. I suppose you haven't seen him, have you, anywhere?'

'No. I haven't seen him since last night. But he's too old to get lost, isn't he?'

'Mr. Hewitt lost two sheep last night.'

'Mr. . . . Well, I don't know who Mr. Hewitt is, but you aren't suggesting, are you, that there's any connection between——'

'The sheep died. They'd been worried by dogs. Two dogs.'

'I see. And did they catch the dogs?'

'They caught one.' Julia frowned, staring absently into the distance. Then her eyes, worried and anxious, met Cliff's. 'He wouldn't, would he?'

'Long John?'

'He wasn't in at all last night,' said Julia.

Cliff had an impulse to warn her that this was the sort of news it was wiser to conceal. The fewer people who knew of Long John's nocturnal adventures, the better, in his opinion. Mr. Hewitt, whoever Mr. Hewitt was, would be glad to pick up a little hint.

'Do *you* think it was Long John?' asked Julia, earnestly.

'Me? I wouldn't know. So long as Mr. Hewitt doesn't think so, I guess Long John's safe.'

'Why would Long John suddenly, if he never had before?' enquired Julia.

'Well, that's how it goes; one moment we're leading a blameless life and the next, we're worrying sheep.'

'I *bet* he didn't,' Julia's voice was fierce. She was struggling off the hammock. 'I *bet* he didn't. I'll go and ask Dominic.'

He watched her swing herself effortlessly from branch to branch of the oak tree; soon, only a flash of skirt and a shoe showed that she was almost at the tree house. Cliff craned his neck, watching, until a sound behind him brought his gaze down again. What he saw brought him slowly and uneasily to his feet.

Simon Wayne was standing near the hammock, staring from it to Cliff. His face was chalk-white and his lips were trembling; by his side, uneasy, puzzled, stood the dog called Long John; Simon's hand was gripping his collarless neck.

'W-where's Julia?' The young voice was hoarse, and Cliff frowned uneasily.

'She was here. She went to talk to your brother, Dominic, up there.'

'Oh. I—I see.'

Simon glanced up; for a moment, Cliff thought that he meant to call his sister, but looked once more at the man standing before him.

'When she comes down, will you . . .' He seemed to swallow with difficulty—'will you tell her that I . . . I found Long John?'

Cliff looked at the dog, and the situation at once became clear. On the animal's mouth was blood; his coat, here and there, was matted and bloody—but the blood was not his own.

'You mean . . . your dog . . . was the other dog; the second dog?' he said, slowly.

Simon nodded. He seemed unable to speak.

'Will you t-tell Julia,' he managed after a few moments,

'will you tell her I'm . . . I'm going to Mr. Hewitt?'

'Oh—but wait a minute!' Cliff put out a protesting hand. 'Now wait a minute! Just because you think——'

'I *know*,' said Simon. 'Don't you see? I *know*. He was out all night. He's never been out all night before—not quite all the night. When I heard about the—the sheep, I felt frightened that it might be . . . but he'd never gone after sheep before, never in his life, and I didn't think he would ever. I looked for him and I found him. He was . . . I think he was hiding. I think he knew.'

'But if they saw the dog who——'

'They only saw one dog. They'—Simon's face turned ashen —'they shot him. Mr. Hewitt shot him.'

'Well, then, what you've got to do,' said Cliff, instantly, 'is to get Long John out of the——'

'I've got to take him to Mr. Hewitt,' said Simon.

'You've . . . you've *what*?' Cliff stared incredulously at the boy. 'You're going to—to take your dog . . .'

'He did it. He was born on Mr. Hewitt's farm. He belonged to Mr. Hewitt once, before I got him. I don't know why he— he went after them, but he did and . . . and Mr. Hewitt's got to know.'

Cliff tried to speak, and found that no words would come. A cry of passionate protest rose to his lips, but he did not give it voice. He wanted to tell the boy not to be a young fool; he wanted to tell him to find a secure hiding-place for the dog and to keep him there until the hue and cry of the search was over. He wanted to explain that a dog was only a dog and needed protection—and forgiveness. And a chance. Blood had been paid for in blood—the blood of the other dog. Long John had escaped and he was entitled to his freedom. A sheep more or less . . . sheep were not pets, they were not dear friends and companions like this dog, pressing against his young master's legs. The duty of a dog owner was to protect his charge against all comers. Simon should learn that. Simon should. . . .

But Simon had turned and was walking steadily away, his

hand on the dog's neck. Cliff watched him for a moment and then found himself stumbling after him.

'Simon!'

Simon turned.

'Look—do you . . . do you have to go?'

The clear grey eyes—Simon's eyes, Dominic's eyes, the eyes of Nicholas—looked up and met his.

'There were two dogs,' he said, 'and the other one didn't get away. . . .'

Cliff had nothing to say. But when Simon went on again, he found himself walking beside him. He had no idea where they were going. He had no idea who Mr. Hewitt was or what would happen when they met him. Above all, he had no idea why his legs were carrying him steadily in one direction while his mind urged him to go swiftly in another. His instincts shouted against going at all; they were marching steadily towards trouble—trouble that could and should have been avoided. He knew that he himself at Simon's age and in Simon's place would without question have kept the dog hidden. He would not be seeking out Mr. Hewitt and risking the loss of the thing he loved best in the world.

But Simon was going—and he was going with him, and he wished fiercely that he had learned to mind his own business and leave the Waynes, young and old, to proceed with theirs. This boy, this white, slim, serious boy walking silently beside him . . . this was his affair, and had nothing to do with chance visitors. The sensible thing would be to let him go on his way and take his dog with him.

Cliff's legs, however, plodded on. He saw Simon glance up at him once, but he kept his gaze steadily ahead. They reached a field and crossed it. They skirted a barn, crossed a farmyard and then, from one of the farm buildings, there emerged a burly man in tweeds and boots and gaiters. Simon halted. The man's eyes swept the boy and the dog, rested for a moment on Cliff and then went inevitably to the clear evidence on the dog's coat.

There was a long silence. The eyes of the two men met, and Cliff became aware that the farmer had known the truth. He had known that Long John was the second dog; no doubt he had seen him—and spared him; why, Cliff could not decide. It might be, he thought, because he felt that the decision rested with Simon.

'He did it, Mr. Hewitt,' said Simon, at last.

His voice was high and thin, but firm.

'Aye. He did it,' echoed Mr. Hewitt. 'There were two of them. They killed two of my sheep—you know that?'

'Yes.'

'Come and look at them,' directed Mr. Hewitt.

They followed him wordlessly to a field beyond the one by which they had come. If Long John's guilt had not been marked in blood upon his coat, his demeanour on reaching the field would have betrayed him. Trembling and terrified, he resisted all Simon's attempts to drag him up to the two sheep lying dead beside the hedge.

'He knows,' said Mr. Hewitt grimly. 'Aye, he knows all right. And he knows something else, too. He knows what happened to the other dog. I shot him. If you have to choose between your sheep and a sheep-killer, you don't wait long to decide.'

'He——' Simon's agonized eyes met the farmer's. 'He never did it before.'

'No. But who's to say he won't do it again?'

There was no reply. Cliff looked from the shivering dog to the trembling boy, and wished he were at the bottom of the broad Atlantic. He looked at the red-faced farmer and to his bewilderment sensed that he was waiting for something. For what? Cliff wondered.

His instinct obeyed the signal before his mind had understood it.

'The other dog, Mr. Hewitt,' he asked, quietly. 'Was it the first time he'd done such a thing?'

'It was not.'

'Then . . . isn't there any way of . . . of punishing Long John —of . . .'

'I can shoot him and take no risks,' said Mr. Hewitt, bluntly, 'or I can show him those sheep and I can give him a hiding of the kind he won't forget so long as he's alive.' His eyes met Simon's squarely. 'Which?' he asked.

Simon said nothing. He surrendered the dog to Mr. Hewitt and watched him as he dragged the fiercely resisting animal to the carcasses.

'You see them, do you . . .' said Mr. Hewitt, between his teeth.

He raised the whip he carried and as the first agonized cry rose from the dog Cliff reached out and swung Simon round to face him and held him with a strong grip on his shoulder. They stood close together, unmoving save for Simon's shuddering as the whip fell again and again and the dog's howls rose and filled the air. It seemed to Cliff that it would never end—and then suddenly there was silence, and Mr. Hewitt was beside them, looking down at Simon.

'That was necessary—you understand?' he said.

'Yes,' said Simon. 'Yes, I understand.'

'Take him home. And don't let him think you were on his side. He's had a lesson and I don't think he'll forget it. He knows me and he knows you; he knows what he did, and he knows we've punished him for it. Call him,' he ordered.

'Long John,' called Simon, quaveringly, and then, with firmness. 'Long John—here.'

The dog came and Simon uttered none of the words of love and comfort and reassurance that rushed to his lips.

'Good-bye, Mr. Hewitt,' he said. 'I'm . . . I'm sorry he——'

'That's all right. He won't do it again, I'll take my oath.'

They left the farmer and the farm and walked back across the field, the dog between them. As they neared the trees surrounding Wood Mount, two figures came racing to meet them, and Cliff and Simon stopped to wait for them. Dominic reached them first, and Julia was close behind.

'Simon,' she cried, 'did you find . . .'

She stopped. Silently she and Dominic took in the situation, and then, with a soft little cry, Julia dropped to her knees beside the dog and put her arms gently around his neck.

'Oh, darling Long John,' she said softly, caressingly. 'You're home again—you're with us, Long John, and it'll be all right.'

Dominic put out a hand and Long John's tongue came out and licked it. Then the dog walked over to Simon and looked up at him. Simon dropped a hand gently on his head and looked up at Cliff.

'Thank you very much for coming with us,' he said.

Cliff did not reply. He turned and walked with them to the house and as they went, he was making a firm resolve. Never again. In future, he would mind his own business and keep out of . . . of everything.

So much for the future. And for the present, he needed a drink. A strong drink. And he was going upstairs to find somebody who would give him one—fast.

CHAPTER EIGHT

R O S E L L E offered him a drink. Cliff had gone upstairs in the hope of seeing Estelle, but she was on the floor above with Lucille, and he had found himself in a little pink and white drawing-room with a little pink and white hostess whose welcoming smile made it impossible for him to make his excuses at once and find his way up the last flight of stairs.

If she thought it a little early in the day for a drink, she did not say so. She led him to a little cupboard, opened it and asked him to help himself. Cliff groped among lemonades, ginger beers, tonic waters, ginger ales, tomato juices, orange juices and grapefruit juices and then shut the cupboard door and told her that he was not, after all, as thirsty as he had imagined.

'I've been with your brother Simon,' he explained. 'His dog's been in trouble.'

'T-trouble?' Roselle stared at him, her blue eyes wide and apprehensive. 'Oh—it wasn't Long John, was it . . .?'

'He went after the sheep. Simon took him to Mr. Hewitt and Mr. Hewitt didn't shoot him, but he gave him the thrashing of his life.'

'Poor—oh, poor Long John!' For a moment, she looked as though she were going to cry, and Cliff watched her reflectively. She was the crying sort, he mused. This Jeff must live a kind of damp life. He had to admit, however, that she would be one of those rare women who cried prettily; if her nose became a shade pinker when she wept, so would her cheeks, and her eyes would look like cornflowers after rain. Robert had told him that she looked like a rose, and so she did. She was not like any of the others . . . unless it were Simon. Those two were the defenceless, the vulnerable members of the family.

'Tell me about Robert,' she asked, as Lucille had done.

'Robert's fine.' He wished Estelle would come downstairs. 'He's . . . oh, well, he's fine.'

'We miss him,' she said. 'It seems much quieter without him, even though he and Lucille aren't here very much. He and my husband and Nicholas like to—to get together. They get on very well. You met Estelle Dryden, didn't you, when she came this morning?'

'Yes. As a matter of fact, I was talking to her in the garden for quite a while—about her aunt. If she's around, there are one or two points I'd like to——'

'She's upstairs, with Lucille. Why don't you go upstairs and see her?'

He went, and he could only hope that his eagerness to go was not too apparent. He found Lucille and Estelle sitting together over a cup of coffee, and Lucille sent him into the kitchen to get himself a cup.

'I hear you escorted Simon to Mr. Hewitt's,' said Estelle.

'I did. I didn't enjoy it. And in my opinion, the trip wasn't necessary, anyhow.'

'Why not?' asked Lucille.

'Because'—it was Estelle who replied—'Mr. Hermann no doubt feels that it would have been better to hide Long John under the floor-boards until the trouble had blown over.'

'All right,' Cliff faced her squarely. 'That's what he does think, this Hermann, whose other name is Cliff. What's wrong with hiding a dog instead of dragging him out there to be shot?'

'Nothing but a small matter of principle,' said Estelle. 'Do you like your coffee black or white?'

'It doesn't matter how I like my coffee,' said Cliff, 'and if I can't issue invitations to lunch at this house, then you can't dish out the coffee; you and I are outsiders, the both of us. What's this principle you spoke about?'

'You needn't get into a temper,' said Estelle, calmly. 'Tempers are the rule rather than the exception in this house. Robert can give some very impressive displays—can't he, Lucille?'

'He can,' said Lucille, 'and my temper's famed throughout the country.'

'It is,' corroborated Estelle. 'And Nicholas can go off the handle whenever he feels like it—so when you glower at us, Mr. Hermann, we don't hide under the sofa; we just glower back. Like this.' She pulled a hideous face and Lucille uttered a protest.

'Estelle—he doesn't look like that?'

'He does—and worse,' asserted Estelle. 'And all because Simon has higher moral standards than he has.'

'The martyr complex,' said Cliff, scornfully.

'You can call it what you like,' said Estelle, 'but it was nothing more than Simon's habit of seeing a thing straight—Long

John was a killer and, therefore, he was as guilty as the other dog.'

'A dog has a right, hasn't he, to claim some sort of sanctuary?' demanded Cliff.

'Christian Churches,' said Estelle, smoothly, 'once afforded temporary sanctuary to those fleeing from the law. The privilege was abolished in the seventeenth century. Anybody claiming sanctuary had to confess his crime and abjure the realm. They——'

'It's the school-mistress in her,' explained Lucille.

'I'm only trying to straighten out Mr. Hermann's thinking, that's all,' said Estelle.

'Mr. Hermann can think for himself,' said Cliff. 'I wouldn't have dragged my dog out there to be shot, and you can make what you like of it.'

'Why didn't you stop Simon, then?' enquired Estelle.

'Because he didn't stop to ask me, that's why.'

'Why did you go with him?'

'Now *that* I don't know,' said Cliff. 'Maybe it was to help him carry back the corpse.'

'Well, it was very kind of you, and we're very grateful,' said Lucille. 'Don't listen to Estelle—she got that trick from her aunt.'

'What trick?' asked Estelle.

'Tearing people's motives to shreds,' said Lucille. 'Cliff, why don't you go out and get your things and pay us a proper visit? You were kidnapped, but I do hope you're not going back to London when you've been to Greenhurst and talked to Uncle Bill. Can't you stay for a while?'

'No, he can't,' said Estelle. 'He says he's got a lot of business to get through. That must keep him in London, because'—she threw Cliff a glance of pure malice—'he can't have any business down here, can he?'

'Will you keep out of this?' Cliff asked her. 'Thank you,' he went on to Lucille, 'I'd like to come and stay if you'll have me.'

'Good. Then why don't you go into Greenhurst now and see Uncle Bill and then go to London and get your things and come back here?'

'I'll do that.' He turned to Estelle. 'How did you get out here this morning?' he asked.

'I got a lift part of the way and walked the rest. If you'll take me back, I'll be grateful.'

'I'll be glad to.'

He followed her downstairs thoughtfully, and they went out to his car. She went inside again and reappeared with Julia's little offering of flowers, and he put her into his car and drove into Greenhurst; as he went, he pondered upon some amazing facts: he had come here less than twenty-four hours ago—unwillingly. He was going to stay—more than willingly. He was driving into a town he had not expected to see again, with a girl he had every intention of seeing again . . . and again . . . and yet again.

He glanced at her and found her studying him with a puzzled look.

'Well?' he asked.

'It's a funny thing,' said Estelle, slowly, 'but you . . . somehow you don't look like you.'

'I don't?'

'No. You're not glowering any more.'

'I'm not?'

'No. I don't want to say anything that might upset you,' she went on soberly, 'but I think I ought to warn you that you look——'

'I look?'

'Almost happy,' said Estelle.

*   *   *

By lunch time, Cliff had seen a good deal of Greenhurst. He had visited the neat little office in which Jeff and his father worked; he had sat in Mr. Milward's quiet room with its windows looking on to the High Street and he had answered his questions about the visit he had paid to Miss Dryden-Smith. He was taken out to a little stone-built cottage and introduced to Jeff's mother. He was taken by Estelle to the newly-painted Travel Agency, where Nicholas received them smilingly.

'So this is where all the great tours get fixed up,' said Cliff, looking round him. 'How's business?'

'Not bad. You'd be surprised to find out how much there is in a small place like this. I do theatre tickets on the side. And all through the summer there are local tours—people like to pile into coaches and drive round the countryside. Where are you two having lunch?' he asked. 'It's almost one.'

'Uncle Bill's giving him lunch at The George,' said Estelle, 'and I'm invited and so are you and so's Jeff. Hurry, Nicholas —I'm starving.'

At the end of lunch, Cliff addressed Estelle across the table.

'I'm driving up to London to get my grips,' he said. 'Would you care to go along?'

'I'd love it,' said Estelle, unhesitatingly. 'Nicholas, his car is like a—a—would I mean leviathan?'

'You might,' said Nicholas. 'Does he drive on the right side of the road?'

'He drives on the left side—when he remembers. Why don't you shut the office, Nicholas, and come too?' she asked.

'Not me,' said Nicholas. 'I've got work to do. I'm starting three old ladies off on a long and expensive Continental tour. They came to the office to ask me to fix them a nice quiet hotel at Torquay—and I've persuaded them that what they really needed was a stimulating look at St. Mark's and St. Peter's.'

'The trip'll kill them all off,' said Jeff.

'Not a bit of it; it'll rejuvenate them,' said Nicholas. 'Estelle, don't get too carried away by large, ostentatious American cars, will you? Beneath the rough interior of mine beats a stout engine.'

'Sure,' agreed Cliff. 'It beat us all the way back from the races!'

'Take no notice, Nicholas,' advised Estelle, and turned to Cliff. 'Before we go up to London,' she said, 'I've got to go home and spend about an hour helping the housekeeper to sort out some of my aunt's things. Will you come up to the house and wait for me?'

So Cliff found himself once more in the drawing-room of the big, red house. But it was no longer neat and orderly; piles of books, piles of gramophone records stood here and there, papers were stacked on the desk; soon, he and Estelle were going on with the work of sorting, rearranging, saving and discarding. They counted and listed heavy silver spoons and forks and miscellaneous articles—salvers, cigarette boxes, ashtrays and candlesticks. Cliff walked over to inspect the pile of gramophone records that had belonged to the dead woman and which represented the careful selection of a lifetime.

'There must be some rare recordings here,' he remarked.

'There are. Patti and Butt and Caruso and Galli-Curci onwards. I thought I'd put the older ones up in the attic and go through them when I've time.'

'Don't you play them?'

'Not much. I like music but I'm not the enthusiast that Aunt Mary was. If she liked a singer or an instrumentalist, she bought every record he made. If she'd been in one of her better moods—when you came that afternoon—she would have made you sit down and listen to all her favourite records. She used to give gramophone concerts sometimes—good ones; people used to come and sit in here and in the dining-room and in the study and at the end of the concert Aunt Mary would give them coffee and sandwiches and then quite frankly tell them to go home.'

'Do you miss her?' asked Cliff.

'I . . . Yes, I do,' said Estelle, slowly. 'But I don't grieve for her, nobody could. She wouldn't want anybody to grieve; she'd think it a great waste of time if they did. You saw her; you know how—how crisp and straight-to-the-point her manner was. She was almost always like that. I know that you come across women like that whose harsh exterior—I think that's the term—conceals a heart of gold. Well ... in Aunt Mary's case, it was more mundane than that. She was, I suppose, the most sensible woman you could ever meet. When I came to live with her, there was never, from the first, any question of being a daughter to her—or of her being a mother to me. She couldn't have been unkind, because good sense doesn't, as a rule, breed unkindness. I was here, she told me, to grow up in a house that would one day be mine. I was—she said—her only living relative; I was to have her house and her money and she hoped to teach me to live with the same prudence and commonsense that she had always lived.'

'But you went out and became a school-teacher?'

'Yes. Perhaps in my own way, I was just as sensible as she was. She thought it foolish of me to work for a degree, and after that to take a teaching post—but I like to think that at the end, when something drove her, when something forced her to change her Will—or to try to—she remembered that I would be all right, that I had a profession and would never— or need never—be unprovided for. But as for grieving for her ... no. I'm grateful to her for what she did for me—but even that's difficult, because she was so careful to instil into me the fact that our relationship was just that and nothing more— kinship. The ties of blood, and not necessarily those of affection. Perhaps that's why I went out and got myself trained to earn my own living—because I felt that there wasn't enough between us to—to even things up. I was taking a lot from her; if I could have given back a little affection ... But she didn't seem to want it.'

'Did you always get on well together?'

'Yes. At least, I grew to understand that forbidding manner of hers, and I learned that if I wanted to do anything for myself, it was wiser to do it first and tell her afterwards; it saved a lot of argument. She couldn't understand why I wanted to do some kind of work—and that's one reason I'm so certain she had no idea of leaving her possessions to this mys-

terious son. If she'd intended it, she would have seen to it that
I could earn my own living—instead of pointing out to me that
I'd never need to. Do you see?'

'Yes, I see,' said Cliff.

He helped her as much as he could with her work of sorting
out and separating and then, when she had done, took her out
to his car and they drove up to his hotel in London. He left her
in the lounge while he packed and sent down his things and
paid his bill; then he joined her with a request.

'Would you mind if we didn't go straight back?' he asked.

'No. Why?'

'Well, I thought we might go along to the nursing home and
look in on those fellow-travellers of mine who got mixed up in
the coach collision. One or two of them are old friends.'

'Didn't you say they were taken to hospital?'

'That's right. But most of us were allowed to leave at once,
and the others moved into a nursing home. Three of them
really needed rest and attention; the fourth guy was all right,
but he's got the kind of nerves that shatter easily. In other
words, he's giving his fans something to sigh about.'

'Is he famous?'

'He's Gonzalez.'

'Manuel Gonzalez? Are we really going to see him?'

'Don't be too eager; apart from his singing, which I'll give
you is great, he's just a big pain. You've heard him sing?'

'Of course. Who hasn't? A good number of those records
you helped me to sort at the Red House were Gonzalez recordings.'

'You like him that much?'

'No; Aunt Mary did. Was he badly hurt?'

'He wasn't really hurt at all, but you couldn't expect him to
miss an opportunity of frightening his public.'

'Who else is at the nursing home?'

'A professsor who was once at school with me. Name of
Tolberge. Nuclear scientist.'

'Who else?'

'The violinist, Escramas. You've heard him, too, of course?'

'Of course. What happened to him?'

'He got his fingers hurt, and so did Gonzalez's accompanist. There was a day or two when they thought the accompanist wouldn't get the use of his fingers back—but both he and Escramas are all right now.'

'I'm glad. They're over here to play at the London Festival, aren't they?'

'Yes. All in all, the coach was carrying an expensive cargo: singers and dancers and musicians—and me. Now come on and we'll buy some flowers for these guys.'

'Or some fruit.'

When they walked up the steps of the nursing home, they were carrying both, and Estelle peered at Cliff over a mass of carnations.

'I feel like a prima donna making my positively-the-last appearance.'

He shook his head.

'Bad casting,' he said. 'You look like the bride.'

They went first into room number twelve to see the Professor. Cliff knocked on the door and looked in.

'Hello, there, Professor,' he said. 'How're you doing?'

'I'm doing fine. Come on in, Cliff,' he invited. 'Come in and sit down.'

'This is Miss Dryden. Estelle, this is one of those guys who's keeping busy putting science to the wrong use. He looks like everybody else right now, but when he gets those bandages off his head, you'll see a noble brow and——'

'Don't listen to him, Miss Dryden. It's very kind of you to come and see me.'

'How long are you going to be here?' asked Cliff.

'Only another two days.'

'Fine; then you can get back to making us more bombs.'

'Don't take him seriously, Miss Dryden. Cliff, have you been in to see the others?'

'No; you're the first. How's the great Gonzalez?'

'Terrible. They'll be glad to throw him out,' said the Professor. 'What he really needs is a nursing home all to himself. There's nothing the matter with him, but he photographs well in pyjamas with flowers stacked round the room and telegrams of enquiry strewn around the bed. He's doing all right; he's making the most of it.'

'And the other two?'

'They're all right, too. The only reason they stayed in was because the doctors were afraid they'd use their hands if they let them out too soon.'

'Will they appear at the Festival?' asked Estelle.

'There's no reason why they shouldn't,' said the Professor. 'I've seen quite a lot of them while we've been here—they come in here to escape Gonzalez, and I've got to know them well. They're an interesting pair.'

'Well, I'd better go and take Estelle to see them—she's wasting her time talking to an obscure guy like you. She wants to see the big shots. Come on, come on,' he urged Estelle. 'Where's Gonzalez—number thirteen?' he asked the Professor as they went out.

'Yes.'

'Then we'll leave number thirteen to the last,' said Cliff, leading Estelle past the door. 'We won't be able to stand too much of Gonzalez and we can make the excuse that we've got to leave. We'll do Escramas next.'

But when they entered the room occupied by the famous violinist, two men were present. Escramas was half-sitting, half lying on the bed, and on a chair by the window was a short stout man in a dressing-gown.

'Estelle, this is the world-famous Escramas,' said Cliff. 'And this—I know you're accompanist to Gonzalez,' he said to the other man with a touch of apology in his tones, 'but I'm sorry, I don't know your name.'

'Paul Moulin.'

'Paul, this is Miss Dryden. She isn't interested in back page news like you or me; she wants to see Escramas. Paul,' he asked, 'tell me something. How do you stand so much of that Gonzalez?'

Paul smiled.

'He is a great artist,' he said, quietly.

'He's magnificent,' said Estelle.

'Yes, he is a great singer,' agreed Escramas. 'One does not think of his idiosyncrasies; one thinks only of his music—is it not so, Paul?'

'It is perhaps sometimes a difficult life,' said Paul, 'but it is never, never dull!'

Estelle watched the two men and smiled to herself at the contrast they presented. Both were Frenchmen, both were about thirty, both were dark and soft-spoken, but there resemblance ended. Escramas was tall and thin, with a long face, black brows and narrow, slanting eyes; he looked more Spanish than French and his lean, supple figure and inscrutable look reminded Estelle of the pictures she had seen of famous matadors. Beside him, the round, rosy face of the accompanist looked almost rustic.

'Are you both quite well again?' she asked.

In reply, both men raised their hands and held them out, flexing the fingers. The long bony fingers of the violinist, the strong broad fingers of the pianist, moved with ease and strength.

'I'm so glad,' she said, gently. 'If anything had happened to your hands . . .'

'If anything had happened to our hands?' Escramas shrugged. 'It is the same in all professions, no? The hands of a musician, or a surgeon, the feet of a dancer, the eyes of a painter . . . the risk is there always.'

'Gonzalez told me you'd never play again,' Cliff told Paul, and the stout figure shook with laughter.

'When you know him well, you do not listen to his exaggerations,' he said. 'He is fortunate, Gonzalez, because all his temperament is on the top; all escapes. With Escramas here, it is different—and not so healthy. Everything goes down, down too deep. To let it all escape, as Gonzalez does—that is the better way.' He turned politely to Estelle. 'You live in London, Mademoiselle?'

'No. I live at a place called Greenhurst.'

'And, for the moment, so do I,' said Cliff.

'Greenhurst?' The two men said the word together, and Escramas raised his eyebrows and turned to Paul. 'It is there, is it not,' he asked in French, 'that we——'

Paul turned to Estelle.

'It is perhaps the place where Escramas and Gonzalez are to appear at a charity concert soon,' he said. 'Is there a rather grand lady called—I think—Templeby near there?'

'Lady Templeby? You mean . . . you mean you're coming down to play at the charity concert?' asked Estelle.

Escramas bowed.

'Oh . . . oh, but that's wonderful!' cried Estelle.

'First I appear at the London Festival and then, before going away, I have promised to play at Templeby. It is an important function, I think?'

'Yes. She holds it every year, and makes large sums for charity,' said Estelle. 'I shall look forward to hearing you there.'

She was still pink with pleasure when Cliff ushered her into room number thirteen and brought her face to face with the famous singer in his flower-filled room. The powerful voice met them as they went in, rolled unceasingly over them for the duration of their visit and pursued them even after they had closed the door behind them.

Manuel Gonzalez was not yet forty, but he had fitted into his life an almost incredible variety of experience. He had lived and loved with the lack of privacy popularly attributed to the goldfish, but he showed none of the goldfish's indifference to publicity. He was a public performer in the widest sense of the word. He was not content to be acknowledged one of the world's finest singers; the limelight that played on him when he sang followed him off the stage and into his home, wherever his home chanced to be—for he moved restlessly from country to country.

He greeted Estelle and Cliff with arms flung wide.

'My friends! Come in, come in, I beg! Come in! I have been so lonely, so lonely! Since this morning, nobody has come—nobody! But they have sent tributes, as you see. Cliff, this lady with the beautiful mouth and the smiling eyes—who is she? I must have her near me, and you must sit on that chair by the window. Cliff, what is her name?'

'Estelle. How are you getting——'

'Oh ... it is ter-*eeble*! Cliff, I cannot explain to you how I have suffered here! The doctors! The service! The staff! The food!' The words rose in a dramatic crescendo. 'Oh ... it is incredible!'

'Don't they——'

'Sometimes I think that they are jealous because people only come to see me, and not their other patients, who are not well known, except Escramas shall I say? The incompetence! The insolence! The disturbances! The noise! The confusions!'

'Terrible, hm?' said Cliff, from the comfortable depths of his chair.

' 'Orrible!' Gonzalez shuddered. 'And you know what they have done? They have put me into room thirteen—I did not look as I came in. I said only to them—give me your finest room. When I told them that, for me, thirteen was a disaster, what do they say? They say: Very well, then: change. Change? But to change is to bring worse luck! How, I say to them, if this room is not unlucky, how is it that all these things have happened to me since I came into it? My silk shirts—ruined! My watch, my gold watch—the gift of a king!—dashed to the ground by an incompetent nurse. My monogrammed leather writing case—splashed with some medicine! But I can tell you, I shall have compensation. I shall see my lawyers when I am well enough. I will not be treated like this. I have lost—who can tell what sum in fees? My concerts! My public! My nerves! Think of my——'

'It's tough,' Cliff rose, patted the singer's hand in a fatherly manner and drew Estelle to her feet. 'Now we must go. We're going down to Greenhurst and I understand you're going down there, too, in a couple of weeks.'

'Greenhurst? I have never heard of it,' declared Gonzalez.

'Aren't you appearing at Lady Templeby's concert?'

'Oh ... that! That woman! Such persistence! Such bribes! Such arguments! Such——'

'Well, we must go; we've got to get some dinner,' broke in Cliff.

'The dinners I have missed! The lunches! The receptions! The ...'

'Well, that was that.' Cliff shut the door behind them firmly, drew a deep breath and then looked down speculatively at Estelle.

'How about coming out to dinner with me before going back to Greenhurst?' he asked.

Her refusal was unhesitating.

'No—thank you very much all the same. I'd like to get back. Mrs. Milward will be expecting me—and Lucille will be expecting you.'

'They have telephones.'

'They've also got nice dinners waiting for us.'

They drove back slowly. Cliff spoke seldom and Estelle, glancing at him now and then, saw that he was looking relaxed and even contented. Though silent, he was not in what she was beginning to describe to herself as his moody mood.

'Don't you find it hard going,' he asked, after a while, 'to keep on one sort of terms with the older Waynes, and another with the junior team?'

'No. It might have been awkward if there had been no break in our relationships,' said Estelle, 'but they were away for a year, and when they came back, I had a teaching degree, and so Nicholas jumped on the young ones every time they forgot to address me as Miss Dryden.'

'Why doesn't he go and get himself a job in a big city?' asked Cliff.

'Because if he did, he'd have to take Simon and Dominic and Julia with him.'

'Haven't they got any aunts, uncles? Couldn't Roselle——'

'Roselle has only been married a few months, and can hardly run her own flat and cook for Jeff. She's learning, but she couldn't cope with the three young ones. Lucille and Robert are not at Greenhurst very often.'

'So Nicholas took on the job?'

'Yes. He came back from his National Service and decided to stay at Wood Mount and look after the children.'

National Service? Cliff did not say the words aloud, but he was thinking hard. National Service—that was roughly a nineteen to twenty-one period. If Nicholas was only a year away from his period of National Service, he could not be more than twenty-two.

Twenty-two. . . .

Cliff had not thought about Nicholas's age; he knew now, that if he had done so, he would have remembered that Lucille was the eldest of the family, and that Nicholas could not have been the twenty-six, seven, eight that he looked. He had an air of authority, of maturity, far beyond his years.

But he was twenty-two. And Estelle?

He did not put the question; already he was aware of her quick flash of anger. He longed to ask her age, for he suspected that, just as Nicholas looked older, she looked younger than she really was. But he did not dare ask. This girl drew a line, and if a man put so much as a toe over it, she came at him with teeth bared. She was sitting here beside him waiting for him to put a foot wrong. She knew that he wanted to know her age, and she probably knew why he wanted to know it. And although he had met her only that morning, there was already in his heart a fear of doing, of saying anything that would anger her.

He said no more. He could get the information he sought

from Lucille, or from Roselle. If she were older than Nicholas, and he felt fairly certain that she was, he would be glad—why, he was not prepared to ask himself.

They did not go to Wood Mount; Estelle wanted to be driven straight back to the Milwards. Cliff stopped at the green gate of their cottage, and a tall figure rose from a deck-chair on the little front lawn and, before Cliff could get out of the car, Nicholas had opened Estelle's door and was helping her out. The light from the hall shone out through the glass of the front door and showed Cliff the smile they exchanged. It was merely friendly, but its very casualness brought to Cliff a remembrance of their long years of comradeship, of companionship, and gave him an unfamiliar feeling of loneliness.

He did not get out of the car. Anger was following loneliness; he could feel it surging, and he knew that he was fighting it vainly.

'Won't you come in and see the Milwards?' asked Nicholas.

'It's rather late, isn't it?' said Cliff.

His tone was so brusque that Nicholas looked at him in astonishment. Cliff raised a hand in careless salute and the car began to move.

'Good-bye,' said Estelle.

Cliff glanced at her.

'Good-bye's a long time,' he said, and drove away.

They stared after him and then looked at one another.

'What's wrong with him?' asked Nicholas. 'Did you have an argument?'

'No. He—he gets like that. It's the playwright in him,' said Estelle.

'He's an odd chap, isn't he?'

'I don't know,' said Estelle, thoughtfully.

'Do you like him?'

'I don't know that either. Just as I decide that perhaps I could like him if I knew him better, his eyebrows come down and he looks like a sulky schoolboy.'

'What made it come on so suddenly this time?'

Estelle could have told him, but she said nothing. There had not been many occasions on which she had felt unable to confide in Nicholas—but this was one. She felt unable, or unwilling to explain that Cliff Hermann was angry because he was not getting from her the attention he wanted—or thought he merited. Robert Debrett had sent him to Wood Mount, and as Robert seldom acted impulsively, it was safe to assume that he liked this man and wanted him to be liked by the family. She wanted to say nothing that would prejudice Nicholas against him. He could make up his own mind—and she would make up hers.

'He went off looking like a wet afternoon,' said Nicholas.

'Perhaps he wanted his dinner,' said Estelle, carelessly. 'Come on inside.'

CHAPTER NINE

T H E next day was Sunday, and Cliff, strolling out of his bedroom in the expectation of breakfasting, as before, comfortably alone, opened the door of the dining-room to find all the members of the family seated round the table. He paused on the threshold and Lucille smiled at him.

'I forgot to tell you,' she said, 'on Sundays we all have meals down here together.'

'Coffee? Fish fried, fish steamed?' offered Pietro, appearing from the kitchen. 'Eggs poached, eggs——'

'Same as yesterday, thanks,' said Cliff.

'What Church do you go to?' asked Julia, through a mouthful of haddock.

'I . . . Well, it all depends,' said Cliff.

'What does it depend on?'

'Oh . . . well, on where I happen to be staying.'

'But'—it was Dominic's voice—'you have to have some special one, don't you?'

Lucille came to the rescue.

'You can go to Greenhurst Parish Church with the children, or to the Catholic Church with Pietro, or to the Anglican Church with Miss Cornhill,' she told him.

'Which one are you going to?'

'I'm staying at home. Alone,' added Lucille, before he could speak.

'You can take the children in your car, if you will,' said Nicholas, 'and I'll call for Estelle and give her a lift in mine. We ought to leave the house about ten-thirty.'

Cliff drove to the Church with the three children. He sat between Julia and Dominic in an uncomfortable pew, and they found the right places for him in the prayer book and handed him the hymn book open at the hymn; they peered at him over their clasped hands to measure the fervency of his prayers. In the row in front were Roselle and Jeff and, in front of them, Nicholas and Estelle. Cliff drew up, through the sermon, a series of masterly plans to detach Estelle from the others and carry her off alone.

None of the plans, however, proved practicable. He stood outside with the family after the service and Estelle spoke to him, but, beside her, Nicholas waited to drive her back to Wood Mount for lunch.

A large, smartly-dressed woman came towards them, and, as she paused to speak to an intervening group, Nicholas gave Cliff a brief summary of who she was.

'Lady Templeby,' he said. 'Wife of Lord Templeby. She lives a mile and a half away from us.'

'Templeby? She's the one who's giving that charity concert, isn't she?'

'The very same. She's got a daughter of marriageable age— Miriam Arkwright—be all right if her mother left her alone. There's also a much younger son, Derek Arkwright, who's about Dominic's age and who's Dominic's chief enemy. She—

oh, good morning, Lady Templeby.'

'Good morning, Nicholas. How is Lucille?'

'She's rather too well, I'm afraid. May I introduce a friend of Robert's who's staying with us? Mr. Hermann. Cliff Hermann.'

'Cliff Hermann—the playwright?' enquired Lady Templeby, examining Cliff more closely.

'The same,' said Nicholas. 'Now, if you'll excuse me, I'll leave you two together and take Estelle home.'

'You must come and dine, Mr. Hermann,' said Lady Templeby, with the air of one giving out prizes. 'I must fix a day. But now I want to tell you all my great news.'

They knew her great news, having heard it from Cliff and Estelle; with exemplary politeness and kindliness they stood round as she told them the names of the two great stars of her concert. They gasped at the name of Escramas and all but swooned when Gonzalez was mentioned. Lady Templeby, pleased with the response, looked at Cliff.

'You have heard of them, of course, Mr. Hermann?'

'I travelled over with them from New York recently.'

'You *did*? Why, this is amazing! Well, I shall take no refusals from anybody; you are all to buy tickets for the concert. They're not at all expensive when you consider what people are going to get for their money. Two guineas each; I call it very reasonable. I shall come to-morrow to see Lucille and to bring you the tickets. Good-bye. Good-bye, Mr. Hermann; I shall fix a date for dinner when next we meet.'

She left them, and Cliff drove the children back to Wood Mount to find that Estelle was already there and was to be there all day. He watched his opportunity and cornered her in the kitchen garden as she was bringing in some lettuces for lunch.

'Haven't you been given a job to do?' she asked him.

'No.'

'Then why don't you find one? Pietro and Miss Cornhill need volunteers.'

'I'll do whatever you're doing,' he said, and found her eyes resting thoughtfully upon him.

'You'd have a lot more fun,' she told him, 'if you tried to get to know the children instead of hiding behind trees every time you see them coming.'

'I never hide behind trees.'

'I was speaking metaphorically.'

'So was I.'

'If you won't work, why don't you go upstairs and talk to Lucille?'

'Because I'd rather talk to you.'

'That's very kind, but I'm busy—and Lucille would like company. She's restless, and she's lonely. The baby's two days overdue, according to her calculations, and every day at this stage—so she tells me—feels like six. You could go up there and amuse her.'

He looked down at her and spoke challengingly.

'You're on the dodge, too,' he said.

'What am I dodging?' she asked, calmly.

'Me—I'd say. What's wrong with giving me some of your time?'

'You're here as a guest of the Waynes—and so am I. What do you propose we should do?' asked Estelle. 'Get in a corner and settle down to a nice chat while everybody else gets lunch ready for us?'

'That's a privilege I understand visitors do have.'

'Well, you've been unfortunate in your choice of hostesses.' Her voice was cool. 'Mine have always been glad to have me with them—and given me jobs to do. And now if you'll excuse me, I'll take this in for the salad.'

Left alone, he walked moodily upstairs and knocked on Lucille's door. He found her packing a suitcase, and raised his eyebrows.

'Off to the Stork Club?' he enquired.

She laughed.

'I wish I were. I keep packing hopefully—and unpacking despairingly.'

'Where do you have to go?'

'London. I wanted to go to the Nursing Home in Green-hurst, but Robert wouldn't hear of it. There's a drink in that cupboard if you want one.'

'Thanks.' He inspected it. 'It's a stronger sort than Roselle keeps. Will you join me?'

She shook her head.

'Why aren't you downstairs with the others?' she asked.

He brought his glass over and sat down near her and looked directly at her.

'Estelle sent me up here—to get me out of the way,' he said.

There was a moment's pause.

'Oh! Why did she do that?' asked Lucille, at last.

'She said that I was trying to get her all to myself.'

'And were you?'

'Of course. She's a very attractive girl. Any man would want to get her all to herself. Lucille, how old is she?'

'Didn't you ask her?'

'No. But she's older than your brother, isn't she? She doesn't look it, but she must be more than twenty-two?'

'She's twenty-four.'

He was silent. Twenty-four. She was two years older than Nicholas—and several thousand pounds richer. Two barriers —but if she loved him, not formidable ones. He knew that Lucille's eyes were on him, and before he could stop himself, had put a question.

'How far has it gone?' he asked. 'Between these two, I mean.'

'Why do you want to know?'

'Because I'm interested—why else? She's a . . . she's a girl a man couldn't help growing to . . . like, once he got to know her. It's easy to see what your brother feels about her—he carries a banner with the news splashed on it—but it isn't so easy to see what she thinks about him. I'd say—just looking at it from a completely outside standpoint—that she's got that sisterly feeling that's so fatal to romance—but, if that's so, why does she hold off anybody else who tries to get to know her? A girl either belongs to a man or she doesn't. If she does, you know where you are. If she doesn't, you try to find out.'

'You're too intelligent,' said Lucille, after a moment's thought, 'to have left out the possibility that she doesn't care greatly for your company?'

'She likes my company. She had some of it yesterday—a lot of it. We got on . . . all right. We got on fine. You know how it is when you're with someone who . . . who catches what you say, what you feel . . . who fits in?'

'Yes, I know.'

'Well, that's how it was. But when we got back to the Milwards' house, there's your brother all ready to wrap his doll up in the box and put her away for the night—out of reach.'

'How long are you going to stay with us?' asked Lucille.

He gazed morosely into his glass, and then frowned up at her.

'You want to know something?' he asked.

'Very much. In fact, I think I ought to know.'

'Well, if I thought I'd ever get anywhere with her, I'd . . . I'd stick around. But not on these terms. No, not on these terms. I never had to take turns with another fellow before, and I don't think much of the idea now. I like her. I'm worried to think how much I like her. I couldn't tell you what attraction she has that three dozen other women I know couldn't match, but at this moment, I'd like nothing better in the world than to get her to myself and try to get better acquainted with her.'

'And she won't let you?'

'No. And you know something else? The more I like her, the less she seems to like me. I don't say I'm a lethal dose of charm, and I don't say that women have fallen into my arms every time I looked at them—but for fifteen years I haven't really given the woman question much thought. Now I meet a girl who seems to me to—to have something about her that sticks in my mind, and I can't even get started.' He lifted unexpectedly hurt eyes to hers. 'I—I like her, Lucille. If I thought that she cared seriously for your brother, I wouldn't do more than wish them both well. But if he's just the old school friend, the old playmate, then——'

'Then you wouldn't really worry about Nicholas?'

He stared at her, his face hardening.

'Then I wouldn't worry about any man,' he said, slowly. 'I wouldn't rob the nest—but if this thing is still an open competition, then I'd like to be in on it.'

'You like her as much as that?'

'I like her as much as that. But if you're worried about your brother, you needn't give him another thought. She looks at me now with something at the back of her eyes—something that says she's added me up and found the total doesn't agree. I don't know why I told you. She's your friend and I suppose it's natural you'd want her for your brother. . . .'

He waited, but Lucille did not help him. She sat musing upon his swift, extraordinary, grudging subjugation to Estelle's charm and found herself oddly touched by his confession. Of them all, it was she, perhaps, who knew Estelle best; she could well picture her irritation at Cliff's refusal to find unlimited pleasure in the society of each and every member of the Wayne family. Estelle, warm-hearted Estelle, would not understand a man who did not make himself at once, as Robert had done, one of them. This aloofness, this apparent lack of interest in what was taking place round him would perhaps have irritated observers less partisan than Estelle—but Robert knew him, had known him for years, and had spoken in his letter of the pleasure they would all get from meeting him. If there were nothing but this sullen look, this moody frown, Robert would not have sent him to Wood Mount.

But now he was here, and he was sitting before her and staring into his glass and turning it listlessly in his hands, and he wanted an answer to a question that only Estelle could answer. Lucille knew that she was not in love with Nicholas—but she believed that some day she might be. Robert had said that time would do it; Nicholas himself believed that patience was his best hope. But now there had come into the picture a man who stated openly his intention of making a bid for Estelle's interest, if not her affection—and he was a man who would not be unduly impressed by Nicholas's slight claims. He had known Estelle for less than twenty-four hours, but Lucille knew from experience that love could come suddenly, unexpectedly, and overwhelmingly.

Nicholas—and Cliff.

She found herself praying silently that this man would go away—that he would leave Wood Mount, leave Greenhurst. It was absurd to have this feeling of premonition . . . he was here for a time and he would go away soon and they would forget him. . . .

They were summoned to lunch; Julia came up to get them and accompanied them downstairs, sliding expertly down the broad, smooth banister. After lunch, the children disappeared out of doors and the grown-ups went to help in the kitchen. Cliff, making a perfunctory offer of assistance and, departing in open relief when it was refused, found a comfortable sofa in the study, and here Pietro, coming in to fetch something from a drawer, found him and, forgetting his errand, embarked upon a long and intricate account of his childhood, his boyhood and the love affairs of his youth. Cliff fell asleep in the middle of his adventures with a girl named Juana, and Pietro, only momentarily dashed, tip-toed away and sought a live audience.

It was not until dusk was falling that Cliff at last found himself alone with Estelle. They were in the drawing-room; she was wearing a coat and waiting for Nicholas to take her home. Lucille and Roselle and Jeff had gone to their own parts of the house; the children were in bed, Pietro and Miss Corn-hill out. Nicholas could be heard issuing the night's orders to his younger sister and brothers.

'Will you be coming out here to-morrow? I could come and fetch you,' said Cliff.

She hesitated.

'Thank you,' she said. 'But I'll wait and see. . . .'

'Had a nice day?' he broke in to ask.

She stared at him.

'Very nice, thank you.'

'I'm glad,' said Cliff recklessly. 'I like to see a girl having a good time washing up, and paring potatoes and keeping the kids out of mischief. Perhaps I can see something of you to-morrow when Nicholas is at his office—if his T-model holds up long enough to get him to his office. I——'

He stopped. Her face was white and her eyes were gleaming with anger.

'Go on, won't you?' she requested. 'Go on with your sneers.'

'I didn't sneer. I——'

'You've done nothing but sneer ever since you came here,' she blazed. 'You sneered at Nicholas's car and at the children and at everybody else in the house. You've had a suffering look on your insufferable face ever since you arrived. You've been sitting about behaving like a man in a ringside seat at a not-too-good circus. You've——'

'I have not——'

'You've done nothing but try to get me into a corner where you could give me the doubtful benefits of your society without interruption from the family. You've not done one single thing since you came here to give us even a glimpse of what Robert Debrett could have been thinking about when he asked you to come. You——'

'What the hell did you expect me to do? I——'

'You could have done anything—just one or two little kindnesses that wouldn't have caused you any trouble and that would at any rate have given the illusion that you were human.

Pietro talked to you, and you listened without one single spark of interest. He asked you if you'd ever seen his brother's restaurant in New York, and you didn't even hear him—and didn't go to the bother of finding out whereabouts in New York it was. You're the first American Miss Cornhill has ever met, and she's been longing to talk to you, and you've done nothing but look at her as if she were—were part of the furniture. You went up to see Roselle once, and wrote her off as an idiotic little thing playing at housekeeping—which she isn't. She's doing her poor little best to look after her husband and make him happy. You did something kind for Simon and he's adored you ever since, and you haven't even noticed the look in his eyes when he looks at you. You sneer at Julia's affection for me, and that's all you know about her. You won't ever, in all your selfish and in-growing life, see a boy as handsome, as attractive as Dominic Wayne—and you don't even find him worth a second look. All you do is stand about and glower. You look like a spoiled schoolboy who needs his head banged against something hard. You're a member of a great nation, and while you're here, you're its representative, and if they knew what they were doing, they'd keep people like you at home and send out somebody who'd at least make an effort to leave a pleasant impression. They——'

'Have you finished?'

'No, I haven't. I want to know what makes you feel that your society will give a woman more pleasure than Nicholas Wayne's. I want——'

'I'm not your infants' class,' broke in Cliff, 'and I find this all very boring.'

'I'm glad you do,' said Estelle, 'I'm glad you find it boring. I won't bore you with it any more, but I hope very much that it has bored you even a fraction as much as you've bored me. Good night.'

Crash!

That was the door, Cliff realized, staring at it bitterly. And so that was that. He was sneery and selfish and in-growing,

and glowering and spoiled and un-American and boring. Not a
bad record for a short visit. That's what came of a man's
simple desire to get a few words with a girl. Well, to hell with
country frolics; in the morning, he would pack his things, say
his farewells and go back to people and places he understood.
To hell with rustics. To hell with . . .

To hell with school-teachers.

CHAPTER TEN

NICHOLAS found Estelle unusually silent as he drove her
back to the Milwards' house in Greenhurst. They were so
much at home in one another's company, however, that a lack
of conversation indicated ease rather than awkwardness; he
left her to her thoughts and pursued his own in equal silence.

'When do you plan to go back to the Red House?' he asked
at last.

She stirred restlessly.

'I don't really want to go back at all,' she said. 'I've asked
Uncle Bill if he'll put the house up for sale—eventually.'

'It's too big for you,' agreed Nicholas.

'And it's ugly, and it's too near the town. But I dread all the
business of selling and moving, and finding another house or a
piece of land to build on.' She screwed herself round on her
seat to look at him. 'You know, Nicholas, it's all very well for
Uncle Bill to say that those few words Aunt Mary wrote before she died have made no difference to the situation. For me,
they've . . . they've completely changed everything. When I'm
with you, or when I'm talking to Lucille, I can think of the
Red House as mine, and Aunt Mary's money as something I
knew would come to me one day. But when I'm alone . . . and
at night, lying awake . . . I feel that if I got up and walked

through the streets and went to the Red House and let myself in, I . . . I wouldn't find it empty.'

'Spooks?'

'No. Just Aunt Mary herself, sitting in the drawing-room and finishing off that Will and looking up at me and handing it to me and saying, "There; that's what I really wanted. Not you, here in this house, but—him." '

It was like Nicholas, she thought gratefully, to think over what she had said instead of answering with automatic re-assurances. He could be trusted to move round the matter until he saw it more or less from her angle.

'You'll have to decide,' he said at last, 'exactly how you're going to face up to the situation. You can go on for the rest of your life telling yourself that you're an interloper—and that wouldn't be a healthy thing. Every time you opened your purse, you'd say to yourself: "Not mine: his." Once you let it grow into a definite feeling of owning something you feel you've no right to, you'll be heading for trouble.'

'I know. But look at it this way,' pleaded Estelle. 'When Aunt Mary died there was a sort of feeling of expectancy everywhere—nobody really thought that the matter would just . . . just peter out. But it has. It did. The stir and gossip and speculation have died completely away.'

'And a good thing too.'

'Yes—but I'm left with a lonely feeling. Instead of having the town behind me, wondering who this son was or is, where he was or is, I'm left to come into his inheritance—because it *is* his inheritance—without one more word or thought being given to him. He's forgotten. Nobody, in a year or two's time, will be able to give you more than a hazy account of what happened on the afternoon Aunt Mary died. Everybody pinned rather melodramatic hopes on Cliff Hermann's turning out to be the son, and when he was produced and proved to have perfectly good parents of his own, all interest in the matter died.'

'And you've got to let it die too. You've got to put it out of your mind—or decide to do something about it. It's brooding without acting that causes serious trouble. You've got to accept—or act.'

'Act how? Mr. Wylie's merely going on with the clearing-up of the estate. Uncle Bill has no suggestions to offer. Can I go out on a crusade taking with me all Aunt Mary's money and possessions and handing them to the first candidate who can support his claims?'

'No. You can never look for him. Uncle Bill and Jeff and I—with old Wylie's help—sketched out a list of possibilities from your aunt's past—and got nowhere. She could have met, married or mated with anybody anywhere—at any time—in those years before her heart began to give trouble and kept her quietly at home. You can rule out, I think, any hope of this man ever turning up. If he'd known who his mother was, or where she was, there would surely have been some visible link between them—letters, papers, some sort of communication. But there's nothing, and you must be careful not to let your mind run round in useless circles.'

'But . . . but it all seems so—so *inconclusive*!'

'Not when you think about it. We'll probably never know what there was behind her last impulse, but I'd stake anything that it wasn't affection—wasn't love.'

'It might have been. Suppose she looked at Cliff Hermann that afternoon and thought to herself: "My son might have looked like this"?'

'She might think it; she probably did think it; he's a good-looking chap and he's about the right age. She may have been seized by regret—but can you feel affection for somebody you haven't set eyes on for all those years? She couldn't have known exactly what he looked like, so she would have had to fall back on her imagination—and I can't see a direct, sensible woman like your aunt growing so sentimental. Cliff Hermann himself wondered whether his father could ever have crossed her path—he looks very much like his father once looked, I believe—but we found that at no time in their lives could the two have met—and so that's out.'

'I know. You follow a thread—and it breaks.'

'And so, being a sensible girl, you leave threads alone and keep your mind out of these blind alleys. If you feel unwilling to take the whole of your aunt's estate, why don't you kill these qualms for ever by—by using some of her money to open a Children's Home of some kind? A home for little boys whose mothers have mislaid them—how about that?'

She smiled at him.

'That would help.'

'Then go on and do it.' He turned into the lane leading to the Milwards cottage, stopped the car and turned to Estelle. 'And I've another suggestion too,' he added, gently. 'You could turn the whole lot over to Uncle Bill and tell him to open a Fund for this charitable project—and then your mind would be at rest and you could ... Please, please, darling Estelle, will you marry me?'

He had taken her hand and was rubbing it softly against his cheek. His lips touched it, and then suddenly he had relinquished her hand and taken her into his arms and was murmuring softly into her hair.

'You're so lovely, Estelle,' he whispered. 'So lovely. . . . You're so sweet and so soft and so heartbreakingly lovely. . . . Darling Estelle. . . .'

She did not draw away. Quiet and unresisting, she stared into the darkness that lay like a curtain round the car and listened to his voice and felt her throat tighten with regret and pity—for him and for herself. She was here safely in his arms; she was older than he in years, but in nothing else; with him, she could be happy and safe to the end of her days. He was bound up with a thousand happy memories of her girlhood; his sisters were her friends, his home already a home to her. She loved him—so much she could be certain of. She loved his touching combination of strength and gentleness; she loved his patience and his teasing and his laughter. She loved him . . . but not enough. Not enough to meet the strong tide of passion that she could feel as he held her against him. Not enough . . . not enough for this.

'We could be happy, Estelle. We don't need your aunt's money. We've got a home; we'd have enough to manage on until the Agency really begins to pay. It wouldn't be a home all to ourselves, but we both love it, and there'd be lots of room for our children, when they come. We could manage—if you loved me. Do you, Estelle?'

She freed herself and took his face gently between her hands.

'I love you very much, Nicholas,' she said, steadily, 'but I—I don't love you . . . enough.'

'Not yet, perhaps. We've known one kind of companionship for so long that it's hard for you to judge where one kind of affection ends and another kind begins. You're so used to me that . . . that . . .' He broke off and took her wrists and brought her hands down and held them. 'Estelle, have you ever liked anybody—any man—more than you like me?'

'No, Nicholas.' Her voice was firm, her answer unhesitating. 'No, I haven't.'

'I'm not the only man who's wanted to marry you. You've had chances of meeting, and loving, other men.'

'I know. But——'

'Couldn't we become engaged, and see how you felt? You could think of yourself as almost belonging to me—and that would get us off the plane of boy-and-girl and up to the man-and-wife level. You could come to it little by little, testing your reactions on the way . . . couldn't you, Estelle?'

'Darling Nicholas, if I wanted to marry you, wouldn't I know—now?'

'I don't think so,' he said, steadily. 'When I came out of the Army and came home and saw you again, I didn't say to myself at once: I love her. But when I did understand how I felt about you, I realized that I'd been feeling that way for a long time—without knowing it.'

'I'd like to wait, Nicholas—please.'

'I'll wait all my life, if you want me to. But waiting for a girl who doesn't show any sign to the world that she belongs to you—that's a dangerous sport. If all comers have to go round me before they can get to you, they think twice before making the attempt—but if I'm nothing but a man you happened to grow up with, then any stray hopeful can leave me out of the picture and feel they've a free hand. Like this American, for example.'

There was a pause.

'What about him?' asked Estelle, at last.

'What about him? Nothing, except that he spent to-day try-ing to manoeuvre you into a siding. Surely you saw? He didn't trouble much about camouflage. Couldn't you feel his hot breath on your neck?'

'No.'

'Then you must have been too busy to notice. He's had his beetling glance on you all day.'

'I . . . I was rather rude to him,' confessed Estelle.

'Rude? When?'

'In the drawing-room just before we left. He got on my nerves quite suddenly and I——'

'Said your piece?'

'Yes.'

'What did he say—to annoy you, I mean?'

'Nothing. At least, it was more manner than matter.'

'What did you say to him?'

'Everything, I think. I lost my temper.'

'Oh my, oh my,' groaned Nicholas. 'Now he'll go and tell Robert. Funny thing, I was coming round to the idea that he was rather a nice chap. Once you get over being frowned at as though you'd insulted his mother's memory, you feel he's not bad. He doesn't make any marked effort to ingratiate himself with anybody, but there's no reason why he should; politeness is only skin deep, I suppose. But that gives you the example I was looking for, darling Estelle. If you belonged to me—if we were engaged—there wouldn't be any argument between you and any man. I could say: This woman is mine, and—and——' His voice faltered. 'This woman is mine . . . mine. Oh, Estelle, I love you so. . . .'

His lips came down on hers, gentle but firm. When he raised his head, he waited, but she made no sign.

'Will you think of me as you lie in bed to-night?' he asked. 'Will you think of what I want—and whether you can give it to me? We could be married soon and you wouldn't have to go back to the Red House ever again. . . . Will you marry me—soon?'

'I . . . I don't know, Nicholas. Please, please give me time.'

He kissed her and then they walked together up to the softly-lighted door of the cottage. He stood for a moment looking down at her.

'Will you be coming out to Wood Mount to-morrow?' he asked.

'I . . . No, I don't think so.'

'Have you so much to do? Couldn't you leave everything and give Lucille as much time as possible until the baby arrives? It can't be long now, and the days drag for her. I'll come out and fetch you and drive you out.'

'All right.' If there was reluctance in her tone, he did not notice it.

'Good girl.' He bent and kissed her, lightly this time, and then he was gone—but Estelle did not move for some time. She stood staring out into the black, silent night, her gaze wide and unblinking, as though she wanted to see what lay behind, beyond the darkness. Then, with a little shiver, she turned and went into the house.

CHAPTER ELEVEN

WHEN Cliff Hermann walked downstairs to breakfast on the following morning he did not, as he had resolved firmly the night before, have a suit-case, packed and locked, in either hand. He had not packed, and he had changed his mind about leaving.

If they didn't like him that way, he told himself grimly, going into the kitchen and clapping the astonished Pietro on the shoulder, they could take a look at him in his new rôle of old family friend. If he could write plays, he could act parts, and now watch him: Enter Cliff Goodguy, face split open in good-guy grin.

'Hi,' he greeted Pietro.

'Good morning, good morning. Coffee? Eggs with——'

'You show me where the things are kept and I'll fix my own breakfast,' said Cliff. 'Who was the guy who breakfasted off:

> *Some toast cut into little bars,*
> *Hot coffee and some strong cigars,*

or words to that effect? I'm not a bad hand at cooking, when I'm pushed right up against it.'

'You cook?'

'I can barbecue a steak second to none. Where d'you keep the eggs?'

'No, no, no—sit down here for a minute and I will do it,' protested Pietro. 'Where did you learn to cook?'

'Oh, here and there. Say, you've got a brother who keeps a sort of a restaurant in New York, haven't you?'

'Ah—Giuseppe! I will tell you about him! I will give you the address where he lives. I will——'

By breakfast's end, Cliff had heard the life history of Giuseppe, his wife, his children, his wife's uncle and his uncle's wife. Strolling into the hall, he lit a cigarette and walked into the study, where he found Miss Cornhill making a quiet domestic picture of a sewing woman.

'Good morning,' he said.

Enter Goodguy, smoking. Perhaps the cigarette was a mistake.

'Does my smoke annoy you?'

Miss Cornhill's keen gaze searched for a moment and then returned to her sewing.

'Not at all. If you're looking for anybody, I'm afraid they're——'

'Oh, I'm not looking for anybody! I've just had a very fine breakfast, very fine indeed. Pietro's a fine cook—but perhaps you find some of his more extravagant fancies a little difficult to control?'

'Yes,' said Miss Cornhill, and snipped off a thread neatly. 'Or again, no.'

'Have you ever been to America?'

'No, never. Might I ask you to hand me that basket? Thank you.'

'There used to be a lot of us around here during the war.'

'Yes, that is so.'

Brilliant conversationalist, this woman. He must write in a bigger part for her.

'The two boys are going back to school soon, I understand?'

'To-morrow.'

'Oh. I suppose you miss them . . . in a way?'

'Very much.'

'They're not much different, on the whole, from American children.'

'You know a great many American children?'

'I . . . Well, I come across them, you know, now and then.'

'Simon,' said Miss Cornhill, carefully selecting a reel of cotton that matched the fabric she was mending, 'has taken a great fancy to you.'

'To me? Fancy! I mean—really?'

'You went with him to Mr. Hewitt's.'

'Oh—that!' Modest disclaimer from Goodguy. 'Do you

have a favourite, Miss Cornhill?'

'Yes, I do.'

'And which of them is your favourite?'

Her eyes were raised again, this time even more briefly.

'Nicholas,' she said.

'Oh?'

'I admire him very much,' said Miss Cornhill in her quiet, formal voice. 'A year ago, he had no job and no prospect of one. He could have gone up to London, or gone abroad, to make a life for himself, but he chose to stay here and undertake the responsibility of the three children. I know a great many men'—her eyes went to a point somewhere above Cliff's head—'who would have refused to tie themselves down in that way.'

'It seems to rest very lightly on him.'

'He doesn't carry his feelings on his face, as some people do.'

'I see. Well, I think perhaps I'll go upstairs and see how Mrs. Debrett is getting along.'

'Do.'

Exit Goodguy. That scene wanted re-writing. Well, she'd got quite a lot said in her bunchy-mouthed way—and her eyes filled in a gap or two.

Now where would all those kids be? Outside, perhaps; he'd better go out and find them.

Before he could carry out this intention, however, there came the sound of footsteps approaching the front door, and a peremptory summons sounded. Cliff walked swiftly through the drawing-room into the garden, but before he had gone far, he heard Miss Cornhill's voice calling him.

'Mr. Hermann!'

He turned. She was standing at the window of the drawing-room and behind her Cliff saw with dismay the commanding form of Lady Templeby. At the sight of Cliff, she put Miss Cornhill aside and marched out to greet him.

'There you are!' she said. 'I've brought the tickets.'

'Tickets?'

'I told you about them at Church yesterday. Shall we go up and see Lucille and talk to her about them?'

Lucille's presence, thought Cliff, would be a help. He followed Lady Templeby up to the top floor and they were admitted not by Lucille but by Estelle.

'Oh—good morning. Do come in,' she said. 'Lucille—Lady Templeby's here.'

Lucille rose and managed a fairly convincing look of welcome, and then they sat down and listened politely as Lady Templeby described the arrangements she had made for her charity concert.

'The concert itself will be in two parts,' she told them. 'I've timed it to begin at seven-thirty. Gonzalez will sing in the first half, because he has to go on to a reception in London; Escramas will play in the second half. I hope to have the hall completely filled—all the tickets are sold and I've reserved carriages in all the trains from London to Greenhurst, and also got buses to bring everybody from the station to Templeby. But Lucille, my dear, I want you, if you will, to put up one of the performers for me, as you've so kindly done in the past.'

'Of course,' said Lucille. 'Will they be staying on after the concert?'

'No, my dear; thank Heaven, they'll all go away immediately after the concert ends. It's a great trouble having to put them up overnight, but I've had too much experience of these famous people to take any chance of their not appearing. I don't risk having them crying off at the last moment; no, indeed. I've had too many of their last-minute telegrams. So I invite them down the night before, Mr. Hermann; I give them a magnificent dinner and a comfortable bedroom and then, on the day of the concert, I know where they are. It's the only way to make certain they'll appear. I'm putting up Escramas and Gonzalez, Lucille, but they're bringing their wives and——'

'Wives?' Cliff gave his first sign of interest. 'They didn't have any wives with them when they——'

'Mr. Hermann!' Lady Templeby silenced him with an up-raised hand and spoke indulgently. 'I do not ask questions. I am a woman of the world, and if a world-famous artist tells me that he is bringing his wife with him, I do not enquire too closely into the matter. Escramas told me that his wife was coming over from Paris to join him for the London Festival. "Then bring her, my good Escramas," I said, "bring her. You and yours are welcome!" And I daresay she'll turn out to be his wife—but in the case of Gonzalez, it is better to see, to ask nothing. We all know his reputation; if the price of having him to sing is to receive a somewhat flamboyant woman he presents to me as his wife, then I shall pay it gladly.'

'Simon and Dominic will be at school; I don't think Nicholas will mind your having their rooms,' said Lucille.

'Thank you. But one will do. I will send you the accompanist—Gonzalez' accompanist. I'm afraid I don't know his name.'

Everybody did their best to look gratified, but nobody looked surprised, for it was Lady Templeby's long-established custom to skim the cream and then generously to share out the skimmed milk.

'His name's Paul Moulin,' said Cliff.

'Indeed? Well, I'm sure he'll be quite charming. And you must come and dine, Mr. Hermann. I shall telephone and fix an evening. Well, Lucille, then you'll very kindly have Mr.— I should say Monsieur Moulin?'

'Yes.'

'You'll like him, Lucille,' Cliff rose. 'He's a nice guy. And now, if you'll excuse me, I'll go down and see the children.' He smiled charmingly at Lady Templeby. 'I haven't much longer with the two boys, you know; they're off back to school to-morrow.'

Followed by a bow from Lady Templeby and blank stares from Lucille and Estelle, Cliff went down into the garden and found Julia and Simon swinging together in the hammock.

Dominic, he learned, was as usual aloft in the tree house and there, determined Cliff, he would leave him; he had no intention of swarming up ropes or branches and bringing on his vertigo. Climbing was not in Goodguy's contract.

'Lady Templeby's upstairs, isn't she?' asked Julia. 'Her car's outside. What's she want?'

'She's selling tickets for a show—or something.'

'She always is. Did Miriam come with her?'

'Miriam?'

'Miriam Arkwright. Her daughter.'

'No; Miriam didn't come.'

'I bet Derek Arkwright didn't come either. Derek's her son. He's a bit older than Dominic. He hates Dominic and Dominic hates him. His mother won't bring him because she says he'll get bullied. So she leaves him outside the gate, or in the car—isn't it a scream? Mr. Hermann, do you know a song about the hat me fayther wore?'

'The hat——?'

> ' *"It's been worn for more than fifty years
> In that little isle so green."*

That's all I know.'

'That's too bad,' said Cliff, 'but I can't help you.'

'You write plays, don't you?'

'Yes. But not musical plays.'

'Did you write them when you were at school, or only when you grew up?'

'Only when I grew up.'

'Oh. Some people are quite good at things when they're young, aren't they? We aren't. None of us,' she regretted, 'can do anything. I'd like to sing and play the piano, but I can't, and Simon would like to play the flute because it sounds nice and soft. Nicholas used to play the trumpet, but he doesn't any more—he says it was only when he was young, but he was playing it when he came home last year. He says it's too late for us to be—to be what, Simon? What did he say?'

'Virtuosos.'

'Well, for that kind of thing, you do have to start early and keep going,' acknowledged Cliff. 'What does Dominic want to do?'

'Nothing,' said Simon. 'He says that if you do things, you're made to do them in front of people, and he says he won't be a dog show. I feel like that, too, I think.'

'Doesn't he ever come down off that tree?'

'Yes. When there's a storm. Because of the lightning. When are you going back to America, Mr. Hermann?'

'I . . . I don't know, Simon. I guess I won't make up my mind yet. I'll stick around here for a little while and hope nobody gets tired of having me. How are you going back to school to-morrow?'

'Nicholas puts us on the train at Greenhurst.'

'Well, how would it be if I drove you back there?'

'You mean'—Simon stared at him, colouring with pleasure —'you mean you'd take us?'

'Why not? There's a big car sitting there eating its head off.'

'Oh, Mr. Hermann'—Julia jumped off the hammock to put the question to him at closer quarters, tore her dress in the process, and ignored the mishap. 'Could I come too?'

'Why not?' asked Cliff.

'Gosh! Dominic!' she screamed without warning, and the sound tore through Cliff's ears and made him quiver. 'Dominic! Come down!'

'I suppose,' said Simon, slowly, 'that Long John wouldn't really fit.'

'Into the car? I guess he'd fit all right,' said Cliff, and saw Simon scrambling to his feet, scarlet with delight. 'I'll go and tell Lucille,' he said.

Cliff lit a cigarette and strolled thoughtfully towards the wooded lane beyond the garden. He walked up and down for some time, his thoughts not too clear. He had read his part. Applause. Well, there it was: if that was family life, he'd carved a piece off it this morning. He'd——

A scuffling behind him made him turn; he saw Dominic running up to join him, and the two walked on together.

'If there's room in your car to-morrow, can I take my tool-box back with me?'

'Take anything you want to.'

'Thanks. It's heavy but it's——' His words and his steps halted abruptly and Cliff, stopping beside him and following the direction of his glance, saw that from above the low wall beside which they were walking had appeared the head of a boy. He was staring at Dominic, and Cliff waited for one or the other to utter a greeting—but to his surprise, no word was spoken.

'Who's your friend?' he asked.

'Derek Arkwright.' Dominic's information had an under-current of menace. 'He can't come in here,' he went on, casually, in a louder tone, his words seemingly addressed to Cliff, but his eyes unswervingly on his neighbour. 'I don't let him come. If he comes in, I kick him out. His mother brought him this morning, but he's afraid to come into our house.'

There was a long pause. In the eyes of the boy looking over the wall Cliff saw fear, hatred and unutterable longing. As he watched him, he saw him put his hands on top of the wall and lever himself to a sitting position upon it. From here he looked down at the other two.

'He's pretending to come,' said Dominic, an open challenge now in his voice.

Derek Arkwright swung his legs round and sat still.

'He's afraid,' said Dominic, conversationally, and Cliff saw the boy drop to his feet and stand before them staring at Dominic, and the fear in his eyes was plain to read, but behind it there was now something of desperation.

Derek Arkwright would have given the world and all his considerable share in it to turn and fly from the scene. Behind him lay the towering outlines of Templeby; in it were the powerful figures of his parents. He knew that they had a greater position, more money and infinitely more influence than all the inhabitants of Greenhurst put together. He knew that he had but to run, and he would be safe.

But for most of his twelve years, he had run from Dominic Wayne. He had looked from afar at Dominic and his wide, at one time wild garden; he had watched the tree-house being built; once, when Dominic was far away and strangers had lived at Wood Mount, he had crept secretly up, up to the topmost branches of the great oak tree and seen the wonders of the lofty hideout. He had, on Dominic's return, suffered the penalty and he had resolved never again to risk punishment at the hands of his lifelong enemy. But he longed with all his spoilt and pampered and lonely heart to bridge the gulf that had lain always between him and the younger Waynes. He had slunk many times into their garden and seen them at play; he had watched Long John gambolling among them, he had heard the shouts and the laughter and the wild games into which he had never been admitted. He was lonely and he was desperate; he was tired of his parents, of his far older sister, of the syco-phantic servants and the ordered banality of life at Templeby. He wanted to be one of the Waynes—but the way was barred. Dominic had barred it and was barring it now.

'Get out,' ordered Dominic.

Derek Arkwright tried to move, and found to his astonish-ment that his legs did not obey him. He had wanted to turn and run ... but he hadn't turned, and he hadn't run. He was still here, still facing the handsome, cool, contemptuous Domi-nic. And he became aware, with fear closing in a tight wall round him, that he was going to stay—and fight. It was the end—or the beginning.

Dominic's eyes narrowed, and anticipation made his heart beat faster. The little beast hadn't bolted. Derek Arkwright hadn't run. He was standing there and ... oh, wonder of wonderful wonders, his fists were clenched. He was going to stand. He was going to fight.

He took a threatening step forward and Derek stood his ground.

'I'll give you one more chance,' said Dominic.

Cliff stirred uneasily, his eyes measuring the combatants. Dominic was younger, stronger and infinitely more solid. The other boy was thinner, but taller; he would have the advantage of a longer reach. But he was the only son of a doting mother, and if those expensive clothes, if that well-scrubbed face suffered injury, there would be an enquiry, and Cliff would be called upon to explain why he had allowed violence to be done.

He put out a hand and then drew it back. Derek Arkwright's face was white, but he had been carried—at last—past fear. He was ablaze with hatred and perhaps with hope. There was a mist before his eyes, but out of the mist one thing stood out clearly: Dominic's face.

He hurled himself at it.

It was a fight, all right, thought Cliff, standing well out of the way of flailing fists. It was a whale of a fight. These two had stayed apart too long; they had a big total of scores to pay off.

He heard a yell, and was astounded to find that it had come from his own lips. He was, he realized, on both sides. He was on the side of the fellow underneath—and first Dominic was, and then Derek. There was no skill in this fight; Dominic's early efforts to observe the rules had been submerged by the necessity to save his skin. Derek Arkwright's methods were unscientific—but they were only too effective.

Through the gasps and the scuffles, Cliff heard a sound, and turned to find Estelle, eyes wide with horror, at his side.

With a dismayed exclamation, she took a step forward to place herself between the opposing forces—and found Cliff's hard grip on her arm.

'No, you don't,' he said, grimly. 'You just leave them to it, d'you hear?'

'They'll . . . I came out to find him. His mother's looking for him. Dominic will hurt him! He'll——'

'Dominic's got his work cut out,' said Cliff. 'They're going to finish this thing. You stay out of it.'

Estelle looked at the combatants and shuddered. Dominic's shirt was ripped from his back and his nose was pouring blood. One of Derek Arkwright's eyes was closing; his jacket was torn, his shirt bloody. He was taking a good deal of punishment—and giving as much as he received.

The sound of a car horn broke peremptorily through the woods, and Cliff released Estelle and walked to the edge of the road. Estelle followed him; together they watched the approach of the Templeby Rolls-Royce. At the sight of them, Lady Templeby gave a sign to the chauffeur and he drew up abreast of Cliff. Lady Templeby leaned out and addressed him.

'Oh—Mr. Hermann! I wonder if by any chance you've seen my little son? Julia said that he came this way but I can't see a sign of him.'

Cliff hesitated. Before him was the order, the immaculateness of Derek Arkwright's existence. Behind him, rolling in the mud, Derek Arkwright was fighting a bloody way to manhood.

He smiled at Lady Templeby and raised his hand, stabbed with a lean forefinger in the general direction of Southampton.

'He went thataway,' he said, and stepped back to allow the car to drive away.

He turned to find Estelle staring curiously at him.

'What did you do that for?' she demanded.

'Do what?'

'Tell lies to his mother.'

'Because sometimes women are nothing but a damn nuisance—and this is one of the times. How would you like a woman squawking over you when you're peeling the skin off your best enemy?'

'But you——'

'But you stand aside and let me get back and see the fight,' ordered Cliff. 'If I mind my own business, you bawl. If I don't, you go on bawling. Now you go back to the women, and leave us men to our own concerns.'

He went past her and walked up to the two boys. They were on their feet, breathing noisily, scarcely recognizable. They stood panting for some moments, and then Dominic spoke.

'You want some more?' he demanded hoarsely.

'If you do,' croaked Derek.

Dominic did not answer for some moments. His glance raked his opponent from head to foot.

'What'll your mother say?' he asked.

'Anything she blooming well likes,' came from the heir of the Templebys.

'What you'd better do'—Dominic wiped his bleeding nose with the remnants of his sleeve—'you'd better come with me and get cleaned up a bit.'

'All right,' said Derek.

Dominic turned, and the other boy fell into step beside him. They walked, shoulder to shoulder, up to Wood Mount, saying nothing. Julia met them and stared incredulously at the battered form of her neighbour. Then her gaze went to Dominic.

'What's *he* doing in our garden?' she asked, aggressively.

'He's with me. Now you shut up,' Dominic told her firmly. He led his friend into the house.

CHAPTER TWELVE

IF Cliff had hoped that Estelle would make one of the party driving back with the boys to school, he was disappointed. She stood at the top of the steps with all the others who had assembled to see them off, and as he drove away Cliff met her eyes and found them full of something he could not interpret —he thought it might be a faint distrust.

Large though his car was, it was overloaded on the outward

journey. The luggage compartment was full to overflowing.
The two boys sat in front with Cliff; Julia was relegated to the
back with Long John, two suit-cases and three bulky packages
containing all the things which Miss Cornhill had found when
the suit-cases had been brought downstairs; two pairs of shoes
which they collected from the mender's on the way through
Greenhurst; two large and awkward pieces of carpentry which
Simon was taking back to the school workshop; an expensive
and fully stocked airport under which Derek Arkwright, at the
last moment, had staggered into view, his face, like Dominic's
decorated with sticking plaster. There had been no opportunity to argue as to whether his parents knew he was present-
ing the entire outfit to Simon and Dominic; he had merely
announced to the boys that it was the one they had been talking about, and, with Julia in the car to receive them, pushed in
through the windows the airport buildings, the control tower,
the luggage trolleys, the Customs and Immigration depart-
ments, the weighing machines and a wide assortment of pas-
senger and freight planes. Cliff's view of the side and back
windows was totally obscured, and the two boys half invisible
behind the upturned landing strips. He removed from his neck
and shoulders some of the sharper corners of the buildings,
eased his ear away from Long John's hanging tongue and
wondered what the school authorities would say when the load
arrived.

But when they came to the great iron gates of the school,
Dominic directed Cliff to a smaller gate some distance away;
driving in through this, Cliff stopped at a Lodge, and a bow-
legged little man came out and watched the unloading with an
embittered countenance.

'Wot's it this time?' he demanded. 'Hair-port! What d'you
expec' me to do? Store all that ruddy stuff?'

'Only for a day or so, Horsey,' Dominic told him, un-
moved. 'I'll come down and cart it away bit by bit. They
won't let me keep it if I take it up to the school.'

'An' I should think not,' grumbled Horsefall, who was

officially school handyman and unofficially the boys' store-keeper. 'Blinkin' lot of rubbish that I'd like to use to keep the school fires going. Come on, come on, git it all in, git it all in there.'

The car was unloaded to a grumbling commentary of which neither Simon nor Dominic took any great heed. When nothing but their personal luggage remained, Cliff drove them to the school, said good-bye and found Simon's grey eyes meeting his own shyly.

'When we get home,' he said, 'you won't be there, will you?'

'No, Simon; I guess I won't.'

'Will you . . . will you be coming back one day?'

'If you ask me.'

Simon's smile broke over his grave, oddly mature face.

'Good-bye—and thank you.' He buried his face for a moment in Long John's coat. 'See you soon, Long John,' he said.

The homeward journey was comparatively peaceful. Long John was behind; Julia sat beside Cliff, sometimes silent, sometimes singing fragments of the songs she had picked up. As they neared Wood Mount, she spoke in an unusually dreamy voice.

'I'm glad in a way the boys have gone,' she said. 'I've got some work to do.'

'Work!'

'I'm going to do a bit of poetry.'

'Oh—so you're going to be a poet?'

'No. Oh, no. I'm only going to write one bit, and I'm going to give it in after half-term and try to win the prize for the best poem. If I win it . . .' Her voice trailed off into silence.

'What's the poem about?'

'It's called Spun Gold. That's a nice title, isn't it?'

'Very nice.'

'I got it out of a book.'

'Spun Gold,' repeated Cliff, feeling his way. 'Spun Gold.

That's . . . that's a beautiful way of describing some kinds of
. . . of hair.'

'Yes. It is,' agreed Julia, eagerly. 'That's what it's meant to
be. It isn't,' she hastened to add, 'a *sloppy* poem. It's only a
short one, but if I get the prize, I want to sort of copy the
poem out neatly and—and give it to the person it was meant
for.'

'And who was it meant for—or shouldn't I ask?'

'It doesn't matter, so long as you don't tell anybody. It's for
Miss Dryden.'

'I see. Would you,' he added, after a pause, 'would you like
me to read it?'

'Oh—no! No, I wouldn't like that,' said Julia. 'If it doesn't
get the prize, I'll tear it up because then I'll know it was no
good. It's only if it—if it turns out to be something with a bit
of good in it—then it won't be sort of cheek to offer it to
her—don't you see?'

'Yes, I see. But if you like somebody, and write a poem
which you think will please them, it doesn't matter much, does
it, whether it's a prize poem or not?'

'I think it does,' said Julia, thoughtfully. 'I think it does in
this case, anyhow. I know what you mean—you mean that
what you feel about something is the important thing. Well,
yes—but why should I shove my bit of poetry at Miss Dryden
just because I want her to know I wrote it about her? That
isn't what I want at all. I want to go to her and say "Please,
Miss Dryden, will you keep this poem, because I wrote it for
you." I couldn't do that unless it was . . . was worth giving to
her. At least, I wouldn't want to.'

'You like her very much, don't you?'

'Yes, I do,' Julia's voice had a bugle note. 'I'd die if the
other girls knew—though it doesn't matter much now that
Miss Dryden's not teaching at school any more—but I liked
her the very first day she came into the classroom. I knew her
before, all my life practic'ly, but only as Lucille's friend.
When she taught us, she wasn't a bit like the other awful

mistresses; she really made you sorry when the bell rang at the
end of the lesson. I don't mean that she was just pretty or
anything—it was ... it was something underneath. It was the
way she sounded. It was her eyes, and the way they could look
laughing or angry or sort of twinkling. It was ... oh, everything! I don't suppose you understand.'

'I think I do,' said Cliff, and quoted softly:

> *'Is she not pure gold, my mistress?'*

'Did someone say that?'
'Robert Browning said that.'
'Say some more, please.'

> *'From women's eyes this doctrine I derive;*
> *They are the ground, the book, the academies,*
> *From whence doth spring the true Promethean fire,'*

quoted Cliff.

'That sounds like Shakespeare—is it?'
'It is.'
Julia sighed.
'I like words—don't you?' she asked. 'I mean, I like shut-
ting my eyes and just saying lines out loud. Miss Dryden made
us learn some lines about words—do you know them?

> *'Bright is the ring of words*
> *When the right man rings them.'*

Cliff's voice joined hers, and they spoke the well-known
lines together.

> *'Fair the fall of songs*
> *When the singer sings them.*
> *Still they are carolled and said—*
> *On wings they are carried—*
> *After the singer is dead*
> *And the maker buried.'*

'That's ... that's wonderful, isn't it?' said Julia, softly. 'The sounds sort of going on ... and on ... Perhaps one day I can write sounds that go on.' She looked at Cliff. 'You do, don't you? I mean, your plays.'

'I don't think they'll go on—and on,' said Cliff. 'Or perhaps they'll go on and on and on—on various stages in various parts of the world, but when the audiences get up and go home, I doubt very much whether the bright ring ... goes on ringing.'

They said no more. Cliff drove, steadily, swiftly, thinking of Estelle Dryden, and he knew that the child sitting beside him was also thinking about her.

They got home to find Jeff's car at the foot of the steps, and Jeff himself taking a suit-case from the car. Julia ran into the house and Cliff walked over to Jeff and the latter looked at him with a grin.

'We missed you,' he said. 'Or rather, we missed your nice fast car.'

'For why?'

'I had to drive Lucille all the way up to London.'

'To the Nursing Home?' asked Cliff, with quickened interest.

'Yes.'

'Nicholas Daniel?'

'No.'

'Lil Liza Jane?'

Jeff grinned.

'No. False alarm. They sent her home'—Jeff swung the suit-case—'with luggage. Nicholas was to have gone, but his car played up again. How did the boys like going back?'

'They didn't complain. They took a lot of contraband with them and dumped it with an old guy with cowboy legs.'

'Old Horsefall. Nicholas used to do the same in his day. It's his old school.'

'Is he home now?' asked Cliff.

'No. He's in Greenhurst, watching his car being fixed. He won't trust them to do the job without him—he's a better mechanic than anybody they've got there. I told him I'd drive Estelle back—she's upstairs.'

'Well, there's no need for you to bother. I'll run her back—when she's ready,' said Cliff.

'Thanks. That's very good of you. In that case,' said Jeff, 'I'll run my car into the garage.'

And here, thought Cliff, watching him driving round to the back of the house, here was where a man's luck changed. Here was the first break—the opportunity. Here was a man's hope of getting a little spun gold for himself.

He did not go into the house. He walked into the garden and watched the sun setting beyond the deserted tree-house. He found an old tree trunk lying beside a wall, and balanced himself precariously and lit a cigarette. And it was here, some time later, that Estelle found him.

'What are you doing out here?' she asked. 'There's been a search party out. Lucille wanted you.'

Cliff got carefully up from the trunk and screwed himself round to remove some patches of mud from the back of his trousers.

'I'm sorry about that false alarm,' he said.

'So was Lucille. She was angrier than I've seen her for a long time. It's a pity you missed it—she looks wonderful when she really flies off the handle.'

'So do you.'

'I suppose'—she hesitated—'I suppose I ought to say I'm sorry for calling you names the other evening.'

'Are you sorry?'

'I'm sorry I said so much out loud.'

He dusted a place on the trunk, and after a moment's hesitation she sat down and he stood leaning against the wall looking down at her.

'It's healthy to get things off your chest,' he said.

'No, it isn't. It's impolite and undisciplined. And a waste of breath, too.'

'Not altogether a waste.'

She raised an eyebrow.

'You mean that after a few angry sentences spoken by a woman you hardly know, you became a new man?'

'I mean that I learned something I didn't know before—that I've begun to look outside the way I sometimes feel inside. I know quite well that sometimes things don't go the way I want them to and I know that I don't trouble to hide my irritation. What I hadn't realized was that I give off a glowering effect even when I'm not feeling glowery.'

'It serves as a sort of protection, I imagine.'

'A sort of armour? It isn't very stout armour; some of those shafts you hurled came right through it.'

'You're not trying to represent yourself as a reformed character, are you?'

'I am not. I haven't even acknowledged that anything you said was either accurate or justified. An angry woman throws the first thing to hand—and throws it just where. All I'm saying is that—if I can use a theatrical metaphor—no actor likes being cast endlessly as one type and one type only. He knows he can widen his range—if they let him. He knows that he can play—for example—a genial old friend of the family.'

'But he'd be acting?'

'Why not? If I'd gone about patting the kids on the head here at Wood Mount, you'd never have known the difference.'

'Well, you've been doing some acting in the last two days. How have you enjoyed it?'

'How did I do?'

'Not too badly. I hope it wasn't too great a strain?'

'I learned one or two things.'

'Yes?'

'Yes. Pietro's life story, for one. And I found out that this housekeeper, Miss Cornhill—she's got a lot more intelligence than I gave her credit for.'

'I could have told you that. In your own language,' Estelle told him, 'she never misses a trick.'

'That's what I gathered.' He put her gently aside and made room for himself beside her on the tree trunk. 'Did you know Mr. and Mrs. Wayne?' he asked. 'I mean Lucille's father and mother?'

'Not Mr. Wayne. At least, I don't remember him too well. I knew Mrs. Wayne, but she was a semi-invalid and she wasn't seen downstairs much. Why do you ask?'

'Because, for one pair of parents, they certainly produced a wide variety of kids. I never saw a family so—so——'

'Widely divergent in character and attainments?'

'Thank you, teacher. But that's what they are. You take Lucille, for example—she's assured and high-spirited, while Roselle is——'

'Faltering and low-spirited. Proceed.'

'There's the ugly, half-wild Julia and the beautiful, self-possessed Dominic. There's Simon, who takes responsibility hard, and Nicholas, who takes it lightly.'

'What makes you think he takes it lightly?'

He looked at her.

'Every time I bring up Nicholas, you square up for a fight. Why?' he challenged.

'Because you underrate him.'

'I don't underrate him at all. I think he's a decent, good-looking fellow doing the job he feels he's been selected for. Further than that, at the moment, I'm not prepared to go. He's young—at least, he's very young compared to me. He's twenty-two and I'm twelve-thirteen years older. What you really want from me is a straight admission that he's a better man than I am—and I won't give it to you, because I don't think he is. Now fight.'

'There's no need to fight. You're entitled to your opinion.'

'And I'm entitled to one thing more: I'm entitled to place my credentials before you, side by side with his.'

'I don't in the least see why.'

'I'll tell you why. Because he's in love with you and he has been for a long time. I'm also in love with you, and have been for two days, seven hours and I can't quite figure out how many minutes.'

There was a long silence. Estelle's eyes were on his, calm, cool and searching.

'I believe you mean that,' she said, at last.

'Get this straight, will you?' said Cliff. 'I'm thirty-five, and I know my own mind. I was engaged once, and thought I wouldn't want to be again. I have never, I give you my word, for what it's worth, told any woman, for fifteen years, that I want to marry her. If I said I'd never put in some pleasant hours with women I've met, I'd be lying, and I don't want to lie to you. But I've been a free man, body and mind, until I came here and saw you. I've pushed this thing away because it seemed to me that it . . . that it wasn't going to work out. But coming back to-day, with Julia sitting next to me, I made up my mind to tell you how I feel. I never in my wildest moments as a playwright set a love scene in as unlikely a setting as this one—but I don't often see you alone and I want to tell you while there's time. To-day, driving back, the car was humming with love for you—Julia's pure little passion—and mine. And now I've told you.'

'What do you want me to say?' asked Estelle.

'I don't want you to say anything—yet.'

She looked at him helplessly.

'It's . . . it's fantastic!'

'As how?'

'For one thing,' said Estelle, 'I don't know anything at all about you. You and I . . . we're strangers. We're complete strangers.'

'That's how men and women, man and maid, man and wife start out—as strangers. They meet, and they look, and some-times they pass on and sometimes they don't. Sometimes they fall in love, and sometimes it takes them a long time to under-stand what's happened to them. I liked you from the moment I met you, from the moment I saw you come into the drawing-room that morning.'

'That morning? You make is sound as though——'

'—it belonged to another life? So it does—it belongs to the life I was leading before I came to Greenhurst. It was a pretty good sort of life and I enjoyed it, but I don't want to go on leading it any more—that is, not by myself. When I go back to it, I want to take you with me, to share it. It may seem impossible to you—it seems almost impossible to me—that a man can glance once or twice at a woman and feel his outlook, his plans, his hopes and his heart changing. But it's happened, and there's nothing I can do about it—or rather, there's only one thing I can do about it: I can try to make you feel the same way about me. And I don't see why I shouldn't have as much chance as the next man. I haven't any illusions about myself—or not too many. I've got a short way with people I don't care for; I didn't know, until you told me, that my face had grown to look nasty all of the time—but I can practise grinning in front of a mirror. I'm a grown man and I can support you and I want you—very much.' He paused and looked more closely at her. 'Are you listening to me?' he asked.

'Yes.' Her voice was dreamy. 'Yes, I am. But I'm listening to something else at the same time.'

'Well, what?'

'Hush! Now you can hear it too. That blackbird—see? That little fellow over there.'

Cliff listened to the clear, sweet notes and presently Estelle went on speaking.

'I'd like to be him—he, it,' she said, quietly. 'I'd like to be able to stay here in this garden always, just singing happily like that. Look at him: he's got no problems.'

'It sounds to me as though he's got the same problem as I have. He's busting himself over there trying to prove that he's in love deeply, truly and as far as he can tell, for ever. He's lucky, yes; when he sings to his love, she doesn't hop farther along the branch saying, "I don't know you well enough." Well, if you'll take your attention off the bird, I'll tell you who and what I am, if it'll make you feel any better.'

'Go on,' invited Estelle.

'I belong to an old family; a very old family. It starts 'way back in the mists of antiquity—1877 to be exact—when a 17-year-old German boy called Hans Hermann hopped on a ship at Hamburg—as a teacher of English, you will mark the alliteration—and went to the United States of America. He was my grandfather. If he had any ancestors, he didn't take their names and addresses with him. He only had one talent—sailing—and he saved up and got himself a boat and from then on he was available for any fishy enterprise being cooked up between New England and Florida. If you wanted anything done just off the land, and just outside the law, you handed the assignment to Hans Hermann. He got rich—naturally—and he died respected, which is harder to understand. But there hasn't been a sea-going Hermann since his day, so maybe we learned when enough was enough. My father turned a small fortune into a large one and handed it on to me. I wrote a play, sold it and haven't looked back since. That's all. I don't see how all that information helps you to love me, but it's yours if you need it. Which brings me to enquire whether you ever heard of any of my plays?'

'I saw the first two; I didn't see the third and last.'

'You liked what you saw? You don't sound enthusiastic.'

'I thought them rather . . . rather too strong for me.'

'Too strong? You mean they couldn't be performed by the Greenhurst Amateur Dramatic Company?'

'They certainly couldn't.'

'I suppose not. It might be dangerous to plop a piece of real life into this pretty little backwater.'

'What makes you think that the people here don't lead what you call real lives? They don't murder one another; they don't ravish one another's wives and they don't use the language of the operating theatre. I suppose that means they're dead?'

'That's fine; get angry.'

'I'm not angry. I just don't understand what's behind your

plays, that's all. They make me feel that it's a waste of time suppressing horror comics. If Simon and Dominic have got to grow up to look at the sort of play and film, and read the sort of book you and your fellow-celebrities are turning out, why shouldn't they be brought up to have the kind of stomach that can stand them?'

'If you don't watch out, you'll topple this tree trunk over and then we'll both be on the ground—the same ground. I'm sorry you don't like looking harsh facts in the face. But life isn't all lived on the level of Wood Mount and a choice of three Churches on Sunday.'

'And this garden isn't all that heap of manure that you see in that corner, either.'

'Why don't you take up dramatic criticism?'

'If I did, you'd be out of a job.'

'Thank you. I'll knock together a little thing called Green is my Hurst, all sweetness and sunlight—that ought to take every manager right by the throat and choke them with their own tears. But I doubt if they'd get their money back on it.'

'So do I.'

'But to hell with commercialism and down with Hermann, yes? You're going to make a fine, helpful wife.'

'I didn't bring up your plays—you did.'

'Well, I'm sorry I did. What happened to that blackbird?'

'Your plays came on, and he left.'

'And that brings me to something else,' said Cliff. 'I'm leaving.'

'Leaving?'

'I didn't detect any regret in that. Yes, leaving. Not leaving Greenhurst—no. No, I'm not leaving Greenhurst—not yet. But I want to, as you'd say, prolong my stay. I want to settle down here for a while—get to know the place, get to know the people, collect some material for my next play—and so on.'

'And so on.' Her tone was sceptical.

'I'm leaving Wood Mount. I'm going to get myself a room at that little hotel, that inn, that pub—what's it called? The

George. I can't go on staying with the Waynes indefinitely—
and there's one Wayne I don't want to stay with. I'm in love
with you and I'm going to do my best to make you love me.
But that's something I can't do under Nicholas Wayne's roof.
So I'm going to move into Greenhurst. How do those lines
go?

> *When captains courageous, whom death could not daunt*
> *Did march to the siege of the city of Gaunt*

—and if you feel that there are few points of comparison between that campaign and mine, define me the word siege,
teacher. Go on define it.'

'It's a . . .' She hesitated.

'And they let you get up there and instruct the young! A
siege, let me inform you, is a nice, long, patient wait around
something that you hope to win. It's a plan to bar all exits
until you can get in there and gain possession.'

Estelle rose slowly to her feet and he got up and stood beside her.

'Why can't you go away—far away?' she asked. 'Why don't
you go away—now?'

'If I did'—he took her face between his hands and held it
firmly up to his—'if I did, would you be glad? Would you—
no, don't move; I'm going to see your eyes and then I'll know
whether you're telling the truth—would you see me go without
one single regret? Would you? Estelle—would you?'

She raised bewildered, unhappy eyes to his.

'In some ways, I . . .'

'Is your heart free and whole and your own?'

'I—I don't know.'

'I think you do know. But you won't listen to your heart—or
perhaps you will, but only to the part of your heart that loves
pityingly—but not passionately. Nicholas wants to marry you.
Given time, he hopes to talk you into it. Given time, he will
talk you into it. But you know, and I know and he knows that
you don't at this moment love him.'

'You're wrong. I don't know it!'

'Yes, you do. But any woman with your warm and generous heart would feel what you're feeling now. You want to give him everything he longs for. You love him too much to want to see him hurt. You'd give anything—short, at present, of yourself—to make him happy. If you could find some good, pretty, suitable girl of twenty or so who loved him and who'd make him a good wife, you'd pray earnestly that he might grow to love her instead of loving you. You want to make Nicholas happy, and Lucille happy, to say nothing of Jeff and Roselle and the whole bunch of them. And the odds are against your holding out too long. The odds are . . . tremendous.'

Estelle said nothing. She could feel only too well the weight of patient, loving pressure. She was alone, and everywhere she turned, she felt the ring of affection closing in upon her. Lucille, Roselle and Jeff, Jeff's parents . . . even the affectionate messages in Robert's letters to his wife. It was a strong current, and unless she decided to leave Greenhurst, to go away, it was bound to carry her to Nicholas. And one part of her heart was willing to be carried—but not the whole.

She stood there without speaking, and Cliff made no attempt to break the silence. For the first time, he felt sorry for her. With all her weapons—wealth, gaiety, humour and charm —she was defenceless against the hope, the loving expectation, that looked out at her from almost every pair of eyes that met hers at Wood Mount and Greenhurst. She was young and alone.

Before he knew quite what he was going to do, Cliff had taken her hand in a firm clasp, and was speaking in his low and steady tones.

'Whatever you want to do, do,' he said. 'Put out of your mind everything but one straight question: Do you, or don't you, love Nicholas enough to marry him? Forget old associations, forget his family, forget your worries about his future happiness. You won't bring him happiness by marrying him because he loves you. That's only the half of it. Forget—until

I remind you—that I love you. Think of one thing only—your own heart. If you ask it a single clear question instead of confusing it by arguing the case for both sides, it'll give you a clear answer. Nicholas has a very potent charm, and you've been under its influence long enough to know whether you're affected by it—or whether time has made you immune. It'll take courage to make you do anything that will hurt this family—but your life is your own and if you can't give your whole heart to Nicholas Wayne, for God's sake don't marry him. If Robert were here, he'd say what I'm saying, once he saw how things were. But with Lucille telling him it's only a matter of time before you fall in love with Nicholas, Robert naturally believes it.'

She looked up at him and he smiled grimly.

'You think I've said all this because I . . . I've got an axe to grind, don't you?' he asked.

Estelle shook her head.

'No. Oddly enough, I don't,' she said, quietly.

'I'll grind the axe later. For the moment, I'll stand on the bank of the stream and if I see you struggling to get out, I'll give you a hand and pull you out.'

'Whichever way?'

'No. Only my way. If you want to get out on the other bank, there are plenty of hands outstretched and ready to haul you in.'

They turned and walked slowly towards the house, but before they had taken many steps, Cliff halted Estelle with a hand on her arm.

'When we go in,' he said, 'I'll be under the roof of the Waynes. But for the moment I can stretch a point and say I'm not—and so I'd be wise to do something I might not have a chance of doing again for a long, long time. . . .'

His arms were round her, and she made no resistance. Her face was lifted to his and her eyes searched his and found in them a deep tenderness and also a steady resolution. His arms his lips were firm and their touch lingering. He released her at last and spoke quietly.

'Now I'm for the city of Gaunt,' he said. 'Good-bye, Estelle.'

A smile, uncertain and tremulous, touched her lips as she gave him back his own words.

'Good-bye is a long time,' she said.

CHAPTER THIRTEEN

IT was almost midnight when Lucille finished her letter to Robert and began to prepare for bed. She undressed slowly, made herself a hot drink and was sitting down to enjoy it when a soft knock sounded on the door and Nicholas put his head round it.

'You in bed?' he enquired.

'No. Come in,' invited Lucille. 'What's the matter with you —sleep-walking?'

Nicholas, in pyjamas and dressing-gown, came in and looked at the half-empty jug on the table.

'It's still hot; you can finish it if you want to,' said Lucille.

'Sure you've had enough?' It was a perfunctory enquiry; he was already pouring the contents of the jug into a cup.

Lucille watched him and waited for him to speak. He was not usually up at midnight. If he went out and returned late or in the early hours of the morning, he went straight to bed and she saw nothing of him; if he was at home, he was usually in bed at this hour. There was something about the studied carelessness of his manner that told her he had something on his mind, and she had enough experience of his moods to know that it would be useless to question him. If he had anything to say, he would say it in his own time.

'Sorry I couldn't run you into the Nursing Home to-day,' he remarked, between sips.

'That's all right. I'm only sorry I couldn't stay there. You feel so idiotic when they smile indulgently and send you home again. Have you fixed your car?'

'Yes. But not in time to run Estelle home.'

'Jeff was going to take her, but——'

'I know; Cliff Hermann offered to go. They went off about nine.'

Nine. And now it was midnight, and it was easy to guess why Nicholas was walking restlessly round the house.

'What's keeping him, d'you imagine?' he asked, with a great show of carelessness.

Lucille hesitated. It was not easy to offer suggestions, the bar of The George would be closed, the older Milwards would be in bed and there was no other place in Greenhurst at which Cliff could be said to be on visiting terms.

'It's not what Robert would call late,' she pointed out. 'I don't suppose Cliff has been so early to bed for years as he's been since he came here.'

It was poor comfort, and what was coming would be poorer comfort still, but she had to say it.

'He came up to see me before he drove Estelle home,' she said.

'Oh? Just to say good night, or something special?'

'He thanked us for having him and said he couldn't, so to speak, trespass on our kindness any more.' She saw the light of hope in Nicholas's eyes and quenched it as mercifully as she could. 'He's moving to The George.'

Nicholas sat for some time before speaking. Then:

'You mean he's leaving Wood Mount and going to stay in Greenhurst. For how long?'

'I don't know. He didn't tell me.'

'I see. As he's staying in my part of the house, couldn't he have told me?'

'He will tell you,' said Lucille. 'He'll tell you in the morning.

But he thought it polite, I think, to come up and tell me first, and I told him he could talk to you about it tomorrow—that is, to-day.'

'You mean'—Nicholas looked directly at her—'you mean you thought I needed some sort of preparation before hearing the news?'

'Why should you need preparation? It wasn't reasonable to suppose he'd stay here for very long.'

'It was reasonable to suppose he'd stay here until he went back to London—or back to the States.'

'I don't quite agree, Nicholas. He's not a country lover. We know that when he came down that afternoon to see Estelle's aunt, he by-passed us; we must have looked altogether too rustic for him. Having got here—having, as it were, been forced to come here, he's had time to find out that there's more . . . that it's more interesting than he imagined.'

It sounded even more unconvincing than she had antici-pated, and she had no hope that he would find comfort in it.

'Lu, what makes you think I'm all that much of a fool?' he asked. 'What could keep him in Greenhurst except Estelle?'

'A lot of things.'

'What things? He's city bred and he admits to liking city lights. He doesn't profess to be a child lover or an animal lover. He doesn't know one plant in the garden from another, he never walks a yard and when he came here, he made it clear that he had a lot of business waiting for him in London. And now he's preparing to fix himself up at The George—because he knows he'll only be five minutes away from the Red House and in a position to drop in on Estelle any time he feels like it. He wants a free hand. You're all out here, Jeff and I are at work. He's been walking round Estelle in smaller and smaller circles ever since he set eyes on her. He's——' He broke off and directed a long, penetrating look at Lucille; 'Has he ever mentioned Estelle to you?'

'I . . .'

He leaned forward and spoke with an odd mixture of urgency and gentleness.

'Lu—don't lie about this. And don't worry about this either. I'm not blind, and I'm not such a blasted fool as to imagine that other men won't see in Estelle everything that I do. This isn't a time for you to have problems on your shoulders. If he's ever given you a hint that he likes Estelle, then tell me. And then forget it. There's nothing you can do about it anyway. If Hermann wants to have a shot at getting to know Estelle better, there's nothing on earth to stop him—except Estelle herself. And if he makes any serious impression on her, I can be quite certain of one thing: that she'll tell me about it. This Hermann may not feel that I'm a factor worth considering—but Estelle does.'

'He does feel you're a—a factor worth considering. That's why he's leaving Wood Mount.'

'I . . . see.'

The colour slowly drained from Nicholas's face and Lucille got out of her chair and went to sit beside him.

'Don't see too much,' she begged. 'I know Estelle as well as you do, but in quite a different way, and surely I'd know, wouldn't I, if she felt attracted by him?'

'Does she?'

'Like you, I feel that if she ever gets to like anybody—seriously—she'll tell us. When we talked about him yesterday, she didn't give the slightest—not the smallest indication of liking him particularly.'

She waited, but to her immense relief, the question she dreaded did not come. Yesterday was yesterday. If Nicholas had asked whether Estelle had spoken of Cliff Hermann to-day . . .

And what, after all, had Estelle said? She had come up to say good-bye before driving home with Cliff, and she had not said anything that could be called definite. But it was this very fact that had roused in Lucille the first real sense of foreboding. If Estelle had only been more at ease . . . if only her manner had not showed a hesitation totally unlike her normal, open, gay, direct self. . . .

'You know, Estelle, don't you,' she had asked when Estelle came upstairs, 'You know that Cliff has decided to stay at The George?'

'Yes. He told me.'

'Did he tell you why?'

There had been, then, the first hesitation.

'Yes. I think it's all rather far-fetched.'

'It's a little . . . sudden.'

'He shouldn't have told you,' said Estelle, suddenly. 'It wasn't right to mention it to you—at a time like this. He ought not to have worried you.'

'Estelle, darling, the thought that Cliff had fallen in love with you, very suddenly but apparently quite seriously, wouldn't worry me. I like him enough to hope that he wouldn't get himself hurt, but I wouldn't worry about his feelings— until I knew, or unless I knew that you returned them.'

There had been no reply. And then for the first time a hand had clutched at Lucille's heart, and Estelle must have seen something in her face, for she spoke in a quick, low voice entirely unlike her own.

'Don't think about it, Lu—please, please don't think about it! If it'll help, I'll tell you that all I feel at this moment is a—a horrible sense of confusion. I can feel myself changing— and I don't know how, or in what way. If Cliff went away now, I promise you that I couldn't tell you, or anyone else, whether I wouldn't give him another thought, or whether . . . or whether he'd take something out of my life with him. I don't *know*, Lucille—I just don't *know*!'

Lucille heard Nicholas speaking, and brought her mind back to the present.

'He shouldn't have mentioned the thing to you at all. He's a selfish hound to have worried you.'

'He did what he felt was . . . honest. Robert sent him here and I'm the person here who in a way represents Robert.'

'You should be kept free from every kind of worry—but I suppose a man who doesn't interest himself in family life wouldn't understand that a woman on the point of having a baby shouldn't be made a repository for his plans—or his hopes.'

'Not exactly on the point of having a baby,' Lucille was glad of a chance to lead the conversation into new channels. 'They said another two weeks.'

'Two *weeks*!'

She nodded dejectedly.

'Yes. Arithmetic was never my strong subject. When I got to the Home to-day, the Matron told me it was nothing but wishful thinking and the doctor said No: wilful thinking. But'—she rose and kissed his cheek softly—'one thing they did recommend was early nights. God bless, Nicholas darling. Go to bed and go to sleep.'

Nicholas went to bed, but not to sleep. In the morning, he rose unrefreshed and in no mood to make it easy for Cliff Hermann to break the news of his departure. He breakfasted early, and alone; he went to the garage and started his car and was debating whether or not to go straight into Greenhurst without seeing his guest, when he saw Cliff Hermann walking into the garage.

'Oh—good morning,' he said.

'Good morning. Can I talk to you for a moment?' asked Cliff.

Nicholas was seated at the wheel of his car; he looked out and answered casually.

'Of course.'

'I was hoping to see you at breakfast. I wanted to thank you for having me here—but the fact is that I feel I can't go on bothering all of you like this any more. I . . .' He looked hopefully at Nicholas. 'I did speak to your sister Lucille about this last night.'

'About what?'

'Well . . .' He knew damn well, thought Cliff, and the too-swift anger rose and was fortunately quelled—'I'd like to stay on at Greenhurst for a little while, but I can't go on staying here and giving a lot of trouble.'

'You're no trouble.'

'You're very kind—but maybe Miss Cornhill wouldn't say it that firmly. I went to The George last night and got myself fixed up with a room.'

'It's just as you like,' said Nicholas. 'You're welcome here as long as you care to stay.'

'Thanks. That's very kind of you. I'm very grateful to you for all you've done. I've liked it a lot being here and meeting you all and getting to know something of the children.'

'Well, if we can do anything, let us know. And now, if you'll forgive me, I'll have to be off; I've got to be at the office early.'

And that, he reflected, driving away, was civilization. Two men talking in polite, albeit somewhat strained tones:

Thanks for everything.

Oh, not at all, not at all. At your service.

I've enjoyed every minute.

So nice of you to say so.

It's been swell.

Do come again

Gee, thanks; I'd sure like to.

And not a word—not a single word on the subject filling the minds of them both. Nothing on the lines of:

Well, I'm getting out, and I guess you know why.

I know all right. You're after my girl, and if you think you've got a hell of a hope——

I'll take my chance. I've got a whole lot more to offer her than you have.

Like what, for instance? Money?

Among other things. I've got my share of looks.

And a stinking temper.

She'll take care of that. I'm as good a man as you are.

Want to prove it? (Draws sword.)

I'll be glad to. (Aims pistol.)

A sword, thought Nicholas longingly. A sword—and the ability to use it. One thrust, and Hermann would be out of the way—for ever. America would not miss one son out of all her millions. Nobody would miss him. And nobody would miss his plays, either, with their preoccupation with tight men and loose women.

If only, if only he had never shown his face in Greenhurst! But the Fates must have been in jesting mood, for Cliff Hermann had not wanted to come. When he had come, that first time, he had driven away with no intention of returning. But Julia had brought him back.

And he, Nicholas, had helped her.

CHAPTER FOURTEEN

GREENHURST thought was slow but tenacious. Cliff Hermann's visit to Miss Dryden-Smith on the afternoon of her death had linked him for ever with her and with the mystery of her half-finished Will. His return to Wood Mount caused no surprise and his move to The George little comment. That Estelle Dryden was in any way connected with his prolonged stay occurred to nobody, not even to Mrs. Ambler, who saw him coming and going constantly to the Red House.

The reason for this lack of perception was not far to seek. Estelle had for years been marked down as belonging to Nicholas Wayne. They had grown up together, and the fact of Estelle's being older by two years was not held to be important; Nicholas was proving himself a man, and a fine one; he had only to pile up a little more money in the till, said local opinion, and then he could claim her. She had enough for two, and Nicholas was too well known and too well liked to be suspected of any interest in her money.

So Cliff went daily to the Red House. Perhaps if he had gone by car, the situation would have become clear to some, at any rate, in the little town. The sight of his big car drawing away just before Nicholas's shabby little one took its place; the fact that the visits of the two men never overlapped; the briefer, less frequent appearances of the little car—all this might have made the situation clearer to those who were interested. But Cliff did not use his car. He used, increasingly, the short field path from the side door of The George to the front door of the Red House. Day by day found him striding over to see Estelle—and when office hours ended and Nicholas was free, Cliff found other ways in which to pass his time. He visited the older Milwards in Greenhurst and the younger pair at Wood Mount. He went upstairs to visit Lucille and Roselle and downstairs to talk to Miss Cornhill and Pietro. His car was often to be seen outside the girls' school, where he would pick up Julia and she would leave her bicycle and go for a drive and sometimes out to supper with him.

Cliff did not know why he spent so much time in Julia's company. It was not, he told himself, for the conversation; they drove sometimes for long periods without exchanging a word. It was not for the pleasure of looking at her : her features, as the days grew warmer, almost vanished under their peppering of freckles. It was not to hear her chant untunefully that

He back, she back, Daddy shot a bear,
Shot him in the back an' he never turned a hair.

Perhaps it was his certain knowledge that during their long silences, the minds of both of them were occupied by thoughts of the same person. When Julia's brows were knit, he could be sure that she had come to a faulty line or a halting metre in *Spun Gold*. When she smiled in the middle of her daydreams, he knew that she had thought of a new line.

Of the poem itself she would not speak. They discussed other poems—but not that one. Cliff could not decide upon the reasons for her reserve; it was perhaps her fear that he would criticize, or even advise. It was to be her own work, her own tribute.

He and Julia were seldom quite alone; Long John, who was not famed for his intelligence, had come by slow degrees to connect the appearance of the large black car with the visits of his new friend. He bounded down the steps, greeted Cliff with yelps of delight and remained close to him throughout his visits. If Cliff and Julia got into the front seats, Long John got into the back. They drove and talked; he panted and rested his chin in a confiding manner upon Cliff's shoulder.

Once Julia took him up to the attic and showed him her collection of books, which now numbered just under four hundred.

'Don't you ever sort them out—weed them out?' he asked.

'I begin to.' Julia fingered a volume lovingly. 'I mean to— then when I start, I can't make up my mind which to throw away.' She curled up on a sunny patch of floor and pushed across a three-legged stool to accommodate Cliff. 'Didn't you keep all your books?' she asked him.

'No; I can't say I did.'

She looked at him curiously.

'Haven't you got any brothers or sisters?'

'Nope; not one.'

'It can't be much fun for only one.'

'I don't know . . . More toys, more attention.'

'That's the part I wouldn't like—your parents wouldn't have anybody else to go on at, and you'd get it all. And at night when you go to bed, it must be awfully lonely with nobody else to go to bed at the same time and call out to you and talk till you go to sleep.'

'What are you going to be when you grow up, Julia?'

'Me? I don't think I can be anything. I'm not awfully good at learning things. I expect I'll just get stuck in an office. If I'd been a bit better to look at, I expect Robert could've got me into acting in films and things, like him, but I'm not photo-photo——'

'—genic.'

'No. It's a pity, because they give you a lot of money. I'd like to get money one day, to help Nicholas. He's sort of been working for us this last year, and Simon says we ought to get jobs one day and sort of get independent. Did you get money after you worked, or did you have it before that?'

'I've never been—short.'

'Well, we have. It's funny, isn't it, how everybody has to get things for themselves? Robert's got lots of money, but Nicholas won't take it. Jeff's father would give Jeff more, but Jeff won't take it. I suppose it's sensible in a way. But what I'd like to do is the sort of thing you don't really get much money for.'

'Writing?'

'Well . . . some sorts. Perhaps not all the time, but I'd like to be able to be quiet like I am when I'm reading up here in the attic or down in the garden—for as long as I want to be—because then I think of words that I'd like to write down . . . sentences . . . and lines of poetry. Not good poetry; not what you'd prob'ly call good poetry, I don't mean, but lines that I think of when I'm . . . when I'm not thinking of anything.'

> *'O for ten years, that I may overwhelm*
> *Myself in poesy'*

quoted Cliff softly. 'Is that what you mean?'

'Yes. Yes, that's just what I do mean. I wish I could have thought of that. Who said that? Shakespeare, I suppose,' said Julia, bitterly.

'As a matter of fact, it was Keats.'

'Keats. You know what he wrote? He wrote my favourite bit of poetry.'

'Good for him. What is it?'

'Ode to Autumn. Only if you say it out loud, I think it sounds much more like summer, because it makes you feel heavy and sleepy—and warm. I don't know where Keats was when he wrote it, but he wasn't at Greenhurst, because here in autumn you forget about the mellow fruitfulness and only think about the mist. It's horrid and cold and damp. But when I feel that I'll never be any good at anything, I say the last verse—you know?

> 'Where are the songs of Spring? Ay, where are they?
> Think not of them, thou hast thy music too.

That's sort of encouraging, don't you feel?'

What Cliff felt was that Julia would never need encouragement. She would go her straight, unswerving way, sometimes seeing her goal, sometimes sensing it—but she would not pause to ask the way or seek help or reassurance. One day she would follow her blunt, freckled little nose to a goal unknown. It would be worth something, Julia's goal.

'Would you like me to read—that is, would it be any help to you if I read *Spun Gold*?' he asked, as he had asked once before.

'No. No, thank you, I don't think so,' said Julia. 'Anyway, it isn't finished yet.'

'When does it have to be given in?'

'This week.'

'And how long do they take to do the judging?'

'The results are going to come out on the same day as Lady Templeby's concert. I thought ... if I won the prize ... I'd stay in after school and copy out the poem properly in a sort of script—my own writing's terrible, but I could do a sort of italics if I went slowly, I think.'

'That ought to look nice.'

'Then I thought I'd buy some red ribbon—very, very narrow red silk ribbon, and I'd roll up the paper to make it look like a—a——'

'Scroll?'

'Yes. And then I'd take it to the Red House and—and tell Miss Dryden I'd got the prize and then I'd give her the scroll and ask her if she'd mind keeping it. Do you think that sounds all right?'

'It sounds very effective to me.'

'Anyway, it isn't even finished yet. If I could stop doing everything else, I could finish it quite soon—but I've got all those other gruesome lessons to think about as well as literature.'

'Don't you like any other subjects?'

'No. I try to, but in the end something goes wrong. I tried to learn geography, f'r instance. The last geography mistress I had—she was a nun in a Convent I was at—taught us about Java, and I learned quite a lot. But when I told the geography mistress in Greenhurst about it, you know what she said? She said it wasn't Java at all; it was somewhere else now. It was In something. Donesia, I think.' Julia frowned hopelessly. 'Honestly, I don't think she even *knows*.'

'The world's changing pretty fast, you know.'

'That's why it's so hopeless to try and learn any geography. And history. . . .'

'You don't like it?'

'Yes, in a way. I could understand it if we just had to learn about the French and the Italians and the Greeks and the Danes—but look at all those other ones: Hittites and Franks and Goths and Visigoths and Berbers and things. I don't know a single thing about any of them and what's more, I don't care—but I've got to go on trying to stuff it into my head, I suppose. What was your favourite subject?'

'I can't remember. Literature, I suppose. And some sorts of music.'

'I like some sorts. I used to like going sometimes to see Miss Dryden-Smith when she was in a good mood. She used to play gramophone records and tell me who they were by and what they were all about. That's why I'm glad Gonzalez is coming down to Lady Templeby's concert. Miss Dryden-Smith had every one of his records. He's got a wonderful voice, hasn't he?'

'Yes, indeed he has.'

'Are you going to the concert?'

'Yes. Are you?'

'Yes. She opens the grounds and part of the house, and you can go in at any time. You don't pay much to get in, but you pay a lot for the concerts. Have you seen Miss Dryden lately?'

'Yes. As a matter of fact, I saw her this morning.'

'She hasn't been to see Lucille so much lately. I expect she's awfully busy clearing up everything that belonged to her aunt.'

'Yes; she's really very busy.'

Julia sighed.

'School's awful without her,' she confided.

Yes, it would be, Cliff thought. To have had Estelle, and to have lost her ... She would be bound up for ever, he was aware, with the sounds of poetry in Julia's mind. The beauty of the words would bring back to her the voice in which they had been spoken when first she had come to hear and to appreciate their beauty. She would see Estelle's face on the pages of a poem; she would carry within her the spark that Estelle had struck.

Estelle. . . .

He had little idea of what progress he was making—or even whether he was making any. He had gained a little courage since he left Wood Mount. Now, when he saw her, he held her in his arms, held her close and kissed her. She did not draw away—but she could not be said to warm under his embrace. Time was passing and the siege was lengthening and he could not decide whether her cool, quiet, steady defences were weakening. Sometimes he persuaded her to drive out with him to near or not so near beauty spots, and sometimes they took their lunch and stayed out until evening.

'Why do you distrust the suddenness of it?' he asked her on one of these outings. 'Why, Estelle? If you looked into the statistics of sudden and slow attractions, you'd find that most people had a pretty good idea, when they first set eyes on someone, whether they liked them or not. "Some day across a crowded room . . ." That makes sense. You see someone—over a lot of other faces that have ceased to mean anything.'

'Don't you want to know something more than just a face?'

'A face can tell you quite a lot. Two people who are spending their lives in some backwater might have time to circle slowly round and look at each other from all angles before coming to a decision—but sometimes you don't get time to do that. You have to trust—you have to take a chance. How long did it take Robert to fall in love with Lucille? Like me, he had to go on, to get out, to get on with his life—and he wanted to take her along. She went.'

'She could come back any time she wanted to. Her home was here. Her brothers and sisters are here. I haven't any home —or I won't have when I give up this one. I haven't any brothers or sisters and I haven't any near relations. I can't——'

'—come back here because it would mean meeting up with Nicholas Wayne again. I know that. But how long do you think these things go on? Will you have to keep out of Nicholas Wayne's life for ever just because you didn't want to marry him?'

'No. And what you're saying is all quite right,' said Estelle, steadily, 'but it leaves out a lot.'

'It keeps in the important point: I love you and I want you to marry me and come away with me. I want you to love me. If you do—once you begin to—you won't ask any more questions.'

'All I——'

'Don't let's talk any more. Come here.' Cliff put out a hand and drew her closer. 'Don't talk. It's too quiet out here to start up any arguments. Put your head against me—like that—and relax. Don't think about anything. Don't think at all. Look up at the blue sky and listen to the larks and just . . . feel. Put your brain to sleep and let your senses have a chance. Here we are—you and I—alone. Are you content here with me, or do you want to get back to town and go on worrying?'

'I like it here.'

'Would you rather be here alone—or with me?'

'With you.'

'Thank you. Now I might be said to be making the first small hole in the defences. An admission like that—even in that cool little voice—is quite something. Do you like my face?'

'When it looks pleasant.'

'Do you like my voice?'

'Yes. Very much.'

'Better and better. Do you want to, to use a laundryism, shrink from me when I touch you?'

'No. At least——'

'You needn't finish that. If I laid more than a forefinger on you, you'd scream for the Greenhurst cop.'

'Policeman.'

'Cop. But I can wait—a little while. And in the meantime, I can kiss you. Is there any law in this country against kissing a school-teacher in the woods?'

'None.'

'Then close your eyes,' he said, gently. 'Go on—close them. . . .'

He could judge a little, take hope a little, from certain signs. She was avoiding Lucille. She saw less of Nicholas. She went far less frequently to Wood Mount and when she went, she did not stay long. She seemed to him to be desperately lonely; he longed to take her away from Greenhurst and break the ties the old association which—he was certain—alone bound her.

He went to the Red House the next day determined to force her to a decision. He found her in the drawing-room, and as he took her into his arms, he saw that she looked tired and drawn.

'Estelle—I want an answer from you,' he said.

She freed herself and walked to the window, as her aunt had done on that day which now seemed years away. He followed her and stood beside her, and they looked out at the warm garden.

'Are you going to marry me, Estelle?' he asked.

'I don't know, Cliff.'

'Do you love me?'

'I don't know. I only know that before you came here, I was happy, and now I'm miserable. Is that love?'

'No, that's not love. That's the state you've got yourself into by trying to hold off love. I would have gone away before this if I'd been sure that you—that you didn't want me . . . but I'm not sure, and while there's a little hope I can't make myself go away. But I think you're clinging to the past. You're clinging to props you don't really need any more. You're holding on to this town, in which you've no real home. You don't like this house; you're just used to it, as you're used to the town and the people in the town. You think that you belong here—but you don't. You've belonged here for one part of your life and—if you can love me—you'll have to leave this and go on to other places—with me. I guess I wouldn't have to say this to you if you really loved me—you'd know it because you'd feel it inside you. But we've got to come to a decision soon, my darling. I've got to go some time—with you or without you. And if it has to be without you I don't know how I'll . . .'

He put an arm round her, and she leaned tiredly against him.

'Why fight like this Estelle?' he asked her gently.

'I'm not fighting.'

'Then why drift like this? You've got a warm heart—but I don't seem to have touched it. If you want me to go away, I'll . . . Yes, I guess I'd go. I thought once that I wouldn't until you came with me. But a man can do so much and then he can't do any more. He can try, and then he finds he's got to the end of his supply of hope. He puts his hopes, his heart, his life, his possessions and his future on a plate and he holds it out—but he can't go on holding it out for ever if the woman he loves doesn't want it. He has to go away, leaving most of his heart behind him, and leave the woman free to—to love somebody else. I've offered you myself; if you don't want me, send me away and I guess I'll—I'll raise the siege and go. Do you want me to go, Estelle?'

There was a long silence.

'No,' said Estelle, at last.

'Do you—love me?'

'I don't know. If I did love you, would I be feeling lonely and miserable and—and wretched?'

'Yes. You'll go on feeling that way until you put yourself and your life and your worries into my hands. You've got to trust me. You've got to believe that the past is over and done with, and that the future's with me. I'm strong. I can hold you up—if you'll only just let me. Don't you see, Estelle? Most of your life you've been on your own, making your own decisions, determined to stand on your own two feet instead of on your aunt's two feet. You grew up with a determination to make your own way and not wait for her to help you—and that's grown to be a habit and now you want to go on standing alone. And because you love Greenhurst and Wood Mount and the Waynes, you feel that you belong to them. But you don't. You belong just wherever your heart is.' He drew her close, and his hold was strong and strangely comforting. 'Won't you try it, Estelle? Won't you! Won't you try to love me?'

He kissed her, and in a quiet helplessness watched a tear trickle down her cheek. He kissed it away, and another came, and then another.

'Don't cry, my sweet,' he whispered. 'Don't cry. You're tired and it's all my fault.'

She put her head against him and gave a long sigh. Her words, when they came, were low but distinct. Cliff heard them clearly but hearing them, stood dumb, unable to comprehend them.

'I love you, Cliff,' said Estelle.

CHAPTER FIFTEEN

LADY TEMPLEBY'S plan of entertaining only the cream of the artistes proved to have certain flaws. Escramas was the first to arrive, and it was found that he had taken his hostess's expansive invitation as a genuine desire to meet his nearest and dearest. He brought his wife, who brought her sister, who brought her husband, who brought their two little girls. The party disembarked at Greenhurst station with numerous cardboard suit-cases, splitting at the seams, and Lady Templeby's overwhelmed chauffeur, after loading the Rolls-Royce to capacity, had to engage two taxis to transport the excess baggage and personnel.

The arrival of Gonzalez was even more distressing. He was not, as everybody expected him to be, accompanied by one of the succession of improbable-looking blondes who swept through his life bringing publicity in their wake; he stepped on to the platform followed only by his accompanist and posed genially for the press. He was then seen to go back to the train and assist from it a small but formidable-looking old woman clad all in black; this, he announced to the crowd assembled to greet him, was his real love, his only love: his mother. He then assisted her reverently into the Rolls-Royce. On arrival at Templeby, his mother listened without comment to Lady Templeby's greeting in the magnificent hall and then inspected her son's room, tested the soundness of the bed springs, insulted the maids and made her way downstairs to assure herself that the chef understood the idiosyncrasies of a great singer's stomach. She sat and wrote diet sheets at one end of the kitchen, while the chef sat and wrote his resignation at the other.

Far removed from this hurly-burly, the quiet and unassuming Paul Moulin was conveyed to Wood Mount and was found to fit into the household, in Julia's admiring words, like a glove. His short, stout form went on noiseless little feet up and down stairs, in and out, as quietly and unobtrusively he made himself known to every member of the family.

His smiling, intelligent, brown eyes took in Lucille's beauty and boredom, and beamed sympathetically upon Roselle's struggles to become a competent housewife. After watching her for some time, he gently offered his assistance, and she found that he was able to do something for her that Pietro, with all his good intentions, had not succeeded in doing: blowing away some of the mists from the mysteries of cooking. Where Pietro had discoursed and gesticulated, Paul instructed and demonstrated.

'Not like that—no,' he said, gently, taking her place at the stove. 'If you will not think me presumptuous. . . .'

'No—oh, no!' The blue eyes filled with tears. 'It's just that I don't seem able to understand what the books—what they want me to do.'

'The books are good, but before the books, there is a little something to learn,' said Paul, in his soft, melodious, infinitely soothing voice. 'I am a Frenchman and cooking, you understand, is—shall we say my heritage? You do not like cooking?'

'I—oh, I hate it.'

'Before I leave this kitchen, you shall like it a little,' promised Paul. This is a challenge to me.' He led her to a little wooden chair and placed her upon it. 'Now,' he began smilingly, 'lesson one: question one: what is food?'

'Food? It's—it's what keeps us alive.'

'Good; very, very good. And since it keeps life in us, we must respect it. This meat that you have treated so cruelly— had you left inside it all its beautiful and nourishing juices, your husband would have enjoyed it very much—and later on, you would know how to cook it for your children so that they would grow strong. This soup—there you have not been cruel, but only a little bit wrong: you have mixed together things which do not like each other.—Do you like music?'

'I . . . Yes, I do, very much.'

'Then try to cook as you would try to conduct. May I use some of these things to show you?'

'Please do.'

'You will have first your solo performer—your important, your principal ingredient. But if he plays by himself, that does not make a symphony, a concerto, you understand? Behind his music, below his playing, there is much more. As a conductor, you will know each note of your score, and you will see that all blends harmoniously. Look at these two things that you put together—they do not like one another. There is dissonance—and indigestion. Since I am only here for one day, shall we together make a meal? The lunch, and dinner too?'

'But—but you're dining at Templeby to-night, aren't you?'

'No.' Paul smiled. 'No, I am not. The great and the famous will be dining there—but the interesting people, the charming people like ourselves, we shall be dining here. Shall we two together cook the dinner?'

'I—oh, I'd love to!'

'And to-morrow morning, if your husband will permit, we shall cook the breakfast, the English breakfast. First I shall work and you shall watch; next I shall ask and you shall answer, and then you will do it alone. We will do only the simplest things—play the simplest music. Here in your pretty little kitchen, you are a magician; a little of this, some of that, the grill, the oven and—wff! a poem, a lyric, sonata. Would you like to learn a little?'

From Roselle to Julia. His first notes on the piano—the aristocratic, once-proud and now neglected and long-suffering piano—brought her to his side.

'You play?' he asked.

'With one finger.'

He smiled.

'Then in that case perhaps the piano is hardly the instrument for you.'

She folded up in her ungainly way and sat cross-legged on the floor beside him.

'Can you play something for me, or is the piano too terrible?'

'The piano is good, but you have not cared for it very well. Is there nobody who plays it?'

'Not really. How old were you when you began?'

'Seven years old.'

'Seven ... If you could count up all the hours and hours you've practised, I suppose it would come to an awful lot?'

'I think so, yes.'

'If you're a good pianist,' Julia asked frankly, 'isn't it better to play at concerts all by yourself, instead of just accompanying someone?'

' "Just accompanying" is not quite right,' said Paul. 'There are many accomplished pianists, but a great many of them cannot accompany. The first time I played for Gonzalez, we knew, both of us, that I could more than just accompany him.'

'But he's'—Julia hesitated—'he's rather a silly sort of man, isn't he? I mean, his singing is absolutely wonderful, but on the station this morning I thought he looked awfully ... spoilt.'

Paul raised his shoulders.

'He is a great artist. He is not easy; no, he is not easy. There are times when I say to myself: No more. But there are many more times when I say to myself: Yes, much, much more of this superb, this incomparable voice, this giant among singers. I feel—almost all the time—humble and privileged.'

'Oh. Yes, I see,' said Julia thoughtfully. 'But if it were me, I think I'd prefer to play on my own. Have you always been everywhere with him?'

'For many years, yes.'

'I'm coming to the concert. We're all going—all except Lucille. She can't go because——'

Julia paused delicately and Paul put on a look of grave understanding.

'You will enjoy that—being an aunt?' he enquired.

'I don't know. I've never been one before. Have you got any children?'

'I am not married.'

'Oh. Did you know that Escramas came this morning with his wife and heaps of other relations?'

'I heard that. But I know also that Lady Templeby was kind enough to invite them.'

'She didn't really mean it.'

'No; she didn't really mean it. Sometimes,' said Paul, 'we are caught like that, no?'

A companionable silence fell. Julia looked frankly at this new friend, readjusted some first impressions: he had an old figure, but a young face; if he weren't short and fat like that, she decided, he'd really be rather nice-looking. She liked the way he used his hands; he did not gesticulate passionately, like Pietro; he seemed rather to fill in his words with the briefest but the most expressive of gestures.

Paul's study of Julia was more veiled, but he spoke of her to Nicholas with some understanding.

'She is interesting, your little sister,' he said.

'Julia?'

'Yes. She has . . . potentialities.'

'She keeps them well hidden,' remarked Nicholas.

'She has a remarkable face.'

Nicholas thought this an understatement, but did not say so.

'She doesn't overwork herself at school,' he said.

'She has no energy to spare to overwork at school,' said Paul. 'She is working all the time—but not at the subjects the school is hoping to teach her. Something is growing, expanding, and one day she will surprise you.'

'She surprises me now,' said Nicholas. 'She can get to the bottom of a class faster than anybody I ever knew.'

Paul laughed.

'You will see—one day.'

'You should read what they say on her reports. If she's got what you call potentialities, why doesn't the school spot them?'

'Because the school is for scholars, and she is not a scholar. She is an artist.'

'She can't play, she can't sing, she can't draw, she can't paint, she can't dance.'

'She can feel.'

Nicholas said nothing. Everybody, he thought, could feel. Why did artists lay claim to deeper feelings than other men? He himself was shaken with feeling now—and he was no artist. Did artists really have a greater capacity for suffering? If they could feel worse than he'd been feeling lately, then he was sorry for the poor devils. Feeling . . . If he told this quiet, soft-spoken Frenchman what he was feeling . . . but he couldn't tell anybody. That, perhaps, was the most bitter part of this particular form of suffering: the necessity for hiding it deep, deep down within yourself. There was nothing to be said, nothing to be done. You stood by and watched another man, a stranger, a newcomer, an outsider . . . you stood and watched him steal your woman away. There was no hope, no redress, no revenge. There were polite congratulations and a heart burning with hate. Who was it who'd called jealousy the injured lover's hell? A poet. An artist. Perhaps they did understand—a little.

But Estelle was going from him. She was not aware, perhaps, that she was changing day by day, becoming more and more wrapped in dreams, less and less the sweet and beloved companion. Her eyes were turning away from Greenhurst and looking towards a future that would be far away from here, far from Wood Mount, far from them all. . . .

And there was nothing to do but wait.

*　　　*　　　*

He would not, he thought, looking at Estelle that evening, have to wait long. If he had doubted, he had only to glance from Estelle to Cliff, who had changed, in these last days, even more than Estelle. He had always been quiet, aloof—now he was even quieter, even more withdrawn, but Nicholas knew that the tenseness that had characterized him recently was gone. There was no sign of joy, or jubilation—but his calmness, his look of peace and tranquillity, told Nicholas all that he had waited, dreaded to know.

He looked round the circle assembled in the drawing-room after dinner. A family circle—or so it would have been once. They were all there, seated in the dusk: Lucille, Roselle and Jeff, Julia, even Long John. Only Simon and Dominic were absent. On the fringe of the circle outside it, sat Cliff Hermann; observers, thought Nicholas, would suppose him to have no connection with the pale girl seated beside Lucille.

Pietro came and went. Miss Cornhill looked in and warned Julia that only a brief interval remained before her bedtime; to-morrow was the evening of the concert and she would be up late; to-night she must be punctual.

But Julia was lying at Paul's feet, and he had transported her from the drawing-room of Wood Mount over the Channel to a warm, wooded village near Bayonne. She could see the trees, the birds, the rose-covered little hotel which had been owned by his father and in which he had been brought up. She was so carried away that it was a shock to find Miss Cornhill addressing her in English instead of French.

'Yes, Miss Cornhill,' she said, absently. 'I won't be long.' She rolled over on her stomach and looked up at Paul.

'Go on,' she begged.

'Where had we come to?' asked Paul.

'Your father and the hotel near Bayonne. Did your mother come from there, too?'

'My mother? No, she did not come from there.'

'Then where?'

Paul smiled.

'Strangely enough, my mother was English,' he said.

'Where did she come from?'

'Come from? Now that,' said Paul, 'is something that I do not know. It is a—what you call a mystery story.'

The low hum of conversation that had been going on round

them stopped abruptly. In the silence that followed, a curious air of expectancy rose and seemed to hover about the assembled company. In the half-light, Cliff's cigarette glowed, dropped and then died as he ground it in an ashtray. Julia's voice broke into the pause.

'Go on,' she pleaded. 'Tell me.'

'But you have to go to bed, have you not?'

'I'll hurry like anything—but tell me first. What's the mystery part?'

'I shall tell you like a bedtime story—and then you will go quickly, eh?'

'Yes. I promise. Go on.'

'Well, my mother came from England, long, long, long ago —once upon a time ago,' said Paul, 'and stayed at a little hotel in the beautiful heart of Provence. I tell this well, eh?'

'Beautifully. Go on.'

'There also my father was staying. He was the nephew of the hotel proprietor, and he was there, as he told my mother clearly, he was there to learn the business—the business of hotelier. His uncle was teaching him, but in between the lessons there was time for other things, you understand.'

'For making love to her, you mean?'

'Yes, that is what I mean. For making love to her. It was summer, and if there were time to tell you before your bath, I would describe to you how beautiful are the summers in Provence. The sun shone, the flowers bloomed, the man and the woman loved.'

'Got married, you mean?'

'That is what I mean. It was perhaps too warm in the sunshine to talk of serious matters like the future, and what should be arranged about this and about that. That was for after. This was the summer, you must remember, and they loved each other very much. And so they got married and they lived happily ever after for the rest of the summer. And then, all at once, the summer was over. My father had to go away, back to his home, and he said Let us go together, and my mother said

No; let me stay here; let us go away from each other and decide whether we really love each other—or whether it was only the sunshine and the flowers. Let us come back in the spring and say the truth to each other—whether it was love for ever, or love in the summer. And so they went away from each other.'

Paul paused, and the artist in him sensed that his audience was with him—an audience wider than the long-legged girl who was following his tale with absorbed interest. Not only Julia, but everybody else in the room was following the story.

'And then what?' asked Julia. 'Did they go back in the spring?'

'Yes. In the spring, they met again, but this time, it was not quite the same. It was a little bit different. Because what do you think was there in the spring?'

'You?' hazarded Julia, after reflection.

'Quite right; there was me. There was this dear little baby of the sunshine and the flowers. You would not perhaps believe this to see me now, but I am told that I was a prince among babies.'

'And then what?'

'And then a lot of things. The first thing was this affair of being an hotelier. That is what my father was, and that is what he was proud to be—but my mother did not seem so anxious, now, to live in France as the wife of a simple hotelier. Let us give up this idea, she said, and live in England. But no, said my father, my life is here—and my son's too.'

' "But he is my son, too," said my mother.

' "He is a Frenchman," said my father—and do you know I think that this gave my mother a great shock. She had not thought, last summer, of having a little Frenchman. They went to my uncle and asked for his advice, but he would say nothing; no, he said, I will not side with this one or with that one.'

'Go on.'

'And I do not know how they would have managed to

arrange something about that, but a more important matter was soon to be decided. This child, said my mother, will belong to the Church of England. This child, said my father, will belong to the Church of Rome.'

'Be a Catholic, you mean?'

'That is right. And upon this matter, my mother and my father forgot all about the flowers and became angry and bitter. And then my mother made up her mind to do what I cannot help thinking to myself was a foolish thing. She decided that she would run away with me. She would kidnap me.'

'Would you call it kidnapping if it was your own baby?'

'Oh, but yes! It is a kid, and you are napping him—so?'

'Did she take you away?'

'She would have done—but now my uncle, who on the subject of nationality had not become very excited, on this subject of religion became very partisan.'

'Very——'

'He would not take sides before, but now he became on the side of my father. And when he understood what my mother meant to do—for all this time she was living in his hotel, you understand?—he went at once to my father and told him the truth. And what did my father do?'

'Ran away with you.'

'Yes. And never, never would my uncle tell where he had gone. My mother came back to England and my uncle never saw her again—but sometimes he wrote to tell her that I was well. One day my mother send money and my uncle sent it to my father, who sent it back to him, who sent it back to my mother—and that was the last time she ever wrote to him.'

'Was that the end?'

'It was not quite the end. When I became a pianist, when I was chosen by the great Gonzalez to be his accompanist, my uncle wrote and told my mother, because he knew she would be proud.'

'Why didn't you ever go to see her?'

'Why? Because for a long time—while my uncle was alive —I knew that he would not tell me where my mother lived. That was the promise he had given my father, before my father died. But a few years after my uncle died, I went to a little village in the Pyrenees to see my aunt, who had gone to live there, and asked her what she knew of my mother.'

'Did she tell you?'

'She could not tell me very much. She had never known my mother's address: she had never known where she came from. She knew only her name, and this she told me.'

'But if she told you your mother's name, you could have come to England and looked for her, couldn't you?'

Paul leaned back in his chair and shook with laughter.

'That was not so easy,' he said. 'It would have been like looking—you know?—for the needle in the haystack.'

'Why?'

'Because——'

The form of Miss Cornhill appeared in the doorway and this time her manner was less genial. Julia got unwillingly to her feet and went out, closing the door slowly behind her and putting her head in to put a last question to Paul.

'What was your mother's name?' she asked.

'Her name was Mary Smith.'

The door closed behind Julia. There was a moment's silence, and then a choking sound, and the violent scraping of a chair—but it was not Estelle who had risen and who stood holding out a hand to Nicholas.

'Quickly—oh, Nicholas, quickly,' gasped Lucille.

*   *   *

Six weeks of rehearsal, Jeff said later, could not have produced more perfect co-ordination. Without fuss, without panic, almost without sound, every man and woman present went into action. Roselle switched on the lights in the hall. Paul and Nicholas supported Lucille outside and down the steps. Jeff vanished and reappeared with her suit-case. Cliff, after one glance at Lucille, waved Nicholas and Paul imperiously away from his car, to which they were leading her.

'Too late for that,' he said, and raced with surprising speed to the huge laundry van which, having delivered the clean laundry, was leaving by the side gate. He held up a hand, halted the van, leapt up beside the driver and directed him to Lucille's side. As the vehicle came to a stop, strong hands seized boxes, hampers, packages of laundry and flung them carelessly on to the drive. Into the empty van Lucille was assisted, and Estelle, racing indoors, came back with a hurrying but otherwise collected Miss Cornhill. She was raised by strong arms and placed beside Lucille; the canvas flap was dropped, the driver sprang to his seat and the laundry van headed at top speed towards Greenhurst.

Nicola Danielle Debrett was born at the junction of the London and Southampton roads, just by the traffic lights. The expensive London nursing home chosen by her father was superseded by the Greenhurst and District Maternity and Nursing Centre, and the gratified laundry company presented Miss Debrett with a year's free diaper service. Rejoicing was universal. The only sour note came from wrathful householders who rang up and demanded the return of their week's washing.

*　　　*　　　*

And in the drawing-room, the last hour of Miss Dryden Smith's life emerged from its fog of mystery.

'But don't you see'—Estelle faced Cliff—'Don't you *see*?'

'I don't see anything. That is, I still don't see any connection between my visit and the fact that your aunt——'

'But it was *you*! She wouldn't ever have known, if you hadn't come that afternoon! It was while you were speaking to her that she learned—without warning, without preparation, without even a chance to—to question you!—what had happened.'

'And what did she hear?' asked Paul, quietly.

'She heard,' said Estelle, 'that her son, Paul Moulin, had been in an accident; that his hand was injured and that he would never be able to play again! Cliff told her that—because he believed it—then—to be true! She asked him about his arm and he told her how it had happened. He told her who the others were—and he told her, he must have told her, because he told me, that you had all believed at one time that you would never be able to use your hand again. Do you wonder she . . . looked ill? Do you wonder she asked Cliff to go, and then stood there trying to make her decision? I leave everything of which I die possessed to my son—to my son, Paul Moulin, who will never be able to earn his living as a pianist again, who is the son of an obscure hotel-keeper, who will live perhaps in obscurity, in despair for the rest of his life—but to whom to save him from this, I will bequeath everything I have. Everything, because there is no time to write more. There is no time to halve, or quarter, or to allocate. There is only time for one short sentence of—of reparation. It was never written, but if any of us believe in an after-life—and I do—we won't care to get to it and meet Aunt Mary unless we've carried out her last will and testament.'

'But no!' Paul recoiled. 'As things have turned out, it is—everything has changed. She acted under . . . it was a mis-apprehension. I do not need, I do not want the money.'

'That has nothing whatsoever to do with it,' Estelle told him calmly. 'You didn't know your mother, but I can tell you—and so can everybody else here—that she was a person who always got her own way. If she didn't, there was trouble. I'm not going to live for the rest of my life waiting to be haunted by the kind of ghost Aunt Mary would be. And if you're wise, Paul, you'll do as she wished—you'll take the money—and put your feelings into your pocket. That's her expression, not mine. If you want to put the money into orphanages, you can; I was going to. Homes for babies whose mothers had mislaid them. . . .'

'I wasn't mislaid,' said Paul, slowly. 'I was——'

'Don't say it!' broke in Estelle. 'You're her son, and she loved your father. You said yourself that you're the child of summer, and sunshine and flowers, and since this is the only thing that's left of that you mustn't ... reject it. I know now that she collected all those records of Gonzalez not to hear him singing—but to listen to you playing. She thought of you as she played the records—and the thought of you was the last thought in her mind when she died. She died writing your name. She died because you came too suddenly out of the past ... hurt and in need. If I ever need money, I shall come to you—but I don't need money. The money is yours; take it, and put some flowers on her grave, and think of her kindly.'

Paul said nothing. He took her hand and raised it to his lips, and Estelle leaned over and kissed his cheek.

'Cousin Paul,' she said, gently.

CHAPTER SIXTEEN

I T was difficult to see Lucille between the floral tributes that had poured in and were still pouring into the Maternity Centre. There were expensive blooms from the theatrical world and homely bunches of flowers from the local tradespeople. Nicholas had come and gone, Julia had inspected her niece and stroked one of its cheeks carefully. Cliff and Estelle met in the corridor and went into the room together, and Estelle sat on the edge of the bed and laid her face for a moment beside Lucille's.

'She's a lovely baby, Lu,' she said, softly. 'Does it feel wonderful?'

Lucille's eyes, quiet with happiness, rested on her.

'Wonderful,' she repeated. 'Robert's pretending he wanted a girl all the time.'

'Have you heard already?'

'Yes. Estelle——'

'Yes, Lu?'

Lucille's glance went to Cliff and then came back to rest on the girl beside her.

'Don't worry about . . . anything,' she said, gently.

A tear rolled slowly down Estelle's cheek.

'A fine thing . . .' She struggled, and produced a smile. 'I came here to—to rejoice with you.'

'Why not let me rejoice with you, instead?'

They looked at one another, and the long weeks of pretence and evasion and dread fell away.

'I love him very much, Lucille,' Estelle said.

'I know. And I'm glad. Robert will be glad, too.'

'Nicholas——'

'Nicholas will be all right—one day,' said Lucille, steadily. 'You can't marry two men, Estelle, darling. Love Cliff and marry him—and be happy.'

'Will you——'

'Look after Nicholas? As far as I can, I will. Now will you go away, darling, and let me talk to Cliff?'

'What do you want to say to him?'

'I want to make him feel that the Waynes would like him to come back—one day.'

Estelle kissed her and rose. Cliff walked with her to the end of the corridor and there, in the shelter of the doorway, he took her in his arms and held her for a moment.

'Bless you,' he said, softly.

She went out into the sunshine and Cliff turned to make his way back to Lucille's room—and then a sound made him pause. It came again—from the bare little waiting-room which they had imagined to be empty. It was not empty; standing near the door was Roselle.

For a moment Cliff stood motionless. He saw, and was not surprised to see, that tears were streaming down her face. The look in her eyes was still one of bewilderment, but her instinct had made known to her the full significance of what she had just seen.

'I'm s-sorry.' She shook the tears away impatiently and struggled to speak clearly. 'I'm so-so terribly sorry. I was c-coming to see Lucille and I couldn't help s-seeing. . . .'

'That's all right, Roselle,' he said, quietly. 'You would have had to know pretty soon.'

She stared at him miserably.

'T-then you . . .'

'Estelle and I are going to be married.'

And then, he scarcely knew how, he had drawn her into the room and closed the door and he was holding her in his arms and she was sobbing against his chest. Cliff, staring over the fair, bowed head and grimly counting the scarlet geraniums growing in the courtyard, patted her shoulder mechanically and made soothing sounds, and came to a firm and unswerving decision.

He would go—at once, and he would take Estelle with him. To be married here in Greenhurst was, as he had known, impossible. If the marriage took place in Greenhurst, the streets of the town would be empty, its inhabitants invisible behind their shuttered houses. The Waynes, if they were in Church, would be in black crêpe. The organ would play a dirge and at the wedding breakfast Pietro would serve husks.

No. He was sorry that it had to be this way, but he was not going to swim to his bride through a lake of local tears. Estelle must come away with him, and she must come to-night. There was only one person besides Lucille who had a right to know their plans, and he himself would see to it that Nicholas was told. He would go to his office and break the news himself and spare Nicholas, and Estelle, the harrowing moments of a last meeting. It was not the way he had hoped to leave Greenhurst —but it was the best, the wisest, the only way. He would tell Nicholas—and Nicholas would tell Julia.

He wiped Roselle's wet little face, at last, with her own inadequate handkerchief. He took her, pale, but dry-eyed and

composed, to Lucille, and afterwards he drove her back to
Wood Mount and left her there.

Long John bounded down the steps and stood beside the
car, his tail wagging wildly, and Cliff opened the door and
leaned out and took the dog's chin in his hand and spoke softly
to the moist, black nose visible through the shagginess.

'Tell Simon,' he said, 'that I'll be back. I don't know
when. Not for years, maybe—but some time. Tell him I
promise, will you? Tell him I'll be back.'

He shut the door and drove away.

*   *   *

The copying out took more time than Julia had anticipated.

It might be, she thought, tearing up the sheet and beginning
laboriously for the third time, it might be taking her all this
time because she was a bit too excited to keep her hand steady.
What with hearing that she'd won the prize this afternoon, and
Lucille's baby being born last night, and Lady Templeby's
concert this evening, things were happening a bit too fast to
keep up with. Life was always like that: absolutely nothing, or
a whole jumble of things coming on top of one another.

If school was always like this—nice and quiet, nice and
lonely—people would be able to learn a bit better. It was nice
to be here all alone, sitting at the desk and feeling wonderful
inside and knowing that even though one reason she'd got the
prize was because all the other poems had been so awful, still
. . *Spun Gold* wasn't bad. It was easy to tell when something
was fairly good that you'd done—you felt all sort of limp when
you'd finished it. Something had gone out of you—and with
luck, it had gone into whatever you'd been writing. If it hadn't,
it was a bit of waste, that's all.

At last the poem was copied out. At last it was done—not
done perfectly, Julia acknowledged, staring at it critically, but
it looked—what Cliff Hermann had said . . . impressive. Only
the finishing touches were needed, and Julia supplied them:
the rolling of the paper into a scroll, the tying with a length of

scarlet ribbon bought—just on the offchance—on the way to
school.

She brushed her hair in the cloakroom, rubbed her hat with
her sleeve and slapped her coat to remove the dust. Then she
went out to the bicycle shed and found to her indignation that
the back tyre of her bicycle was punctured. She pushed
the machine to the High Street and stopped at the bicycle
shop.

'Is it too late to mend a puncture, Mr. Brett?' she asked.

'That depends on what's punctured, Miss Wayne.'

Miss Wayne. They did it mostly for fun, Julia told herself,
but all the same, it was true now; with Lucille and Roselle
married, who but herself should be Miss Wayne?

'It's the back tyre. I could leave it with you and come back
for it later.'

'All right, then. Prop it up there and I'll have it ready for
you in half an hour—at half-past five. How'll that do?'

'Thank you, Mr. Brett.'

She went on to the end of the street, crossed it and was soon
walking up the drive leading to the Red House. She paused on
the doorstep, straightened her hat, gave a hitch to her sagging
underwear and pressed the bell. With her heart beginning to
beat fast, she heard Mrs. Ambler's heavy tread, and a moment
later the door was opened.

'Good afternoon, Mrs. Ambler. Is—is Miss Dryden in?'

'Come in,' said Mrs. Ambler. 'Yes, she's in; straight
through into the dining-room; she's doing some clearing up in
there. Leave your satchel here, won't you?'

Julia shrugged off her satchel, walked to the dining-room
door, knocked timidly upon it and heard Estelle's voice.

Going in, she saw to her relief that no extensive clearing up
operations were hampering Miss Dryden; instead, Estelle was
standing by the window and staring out with what in anybody
else would have appeared to be aimlessness.

'Oh—Julia! This is a surprise—and a nice one,' she said.
'Won't you come in? Or shall we go into the drawing-room?'

Julia advanced, one hand shielding the scroll until she had reached the table and could conceal it beneath its edge.

'I—I can't stay, thank you, Miss Dryden. I just wanted to see you for a minute, to—to tell you something.'

Estelle came forward slowly. She looked at the thin, untidy, familiar figure, the small freckled face and the strands of red hair escaping from the unbecoming school hat. Julia. Julia, who loved her. Julia, to whom she could have been sister, teacher, companion. She could have stayed here watching her grow in mind and body, in grace, in intellect. She would have seen emerging, from this plain awkward child, the fine woman she was destined to become. There would be other Julias across the broad Atlantic, but she would not have memories of them that stretched back to their first day upon earth. They would not have looked up at her from a desk in a classroom, their eyes misted by the beginnings of love.

'Well, Julia?' she asked, quietly.

'I came to tell you . . .' Julia paused and brought it out with a burst. 'I won the poetry prize, Miss Dryden. I did a poem. I gave it in and I thought, in a way, it wasn't bad, because when I was writing it I felt . . . I thought about . . . well, about you, in a way. That's why I've come. I couldn't bring the prize to show you because you aren't allowed to take it out of school, but I thought that if you wouldn't mind taking the—the poem, I'd like you to have it and keep it, if you wouldn't mind, because it was really written for you, in a way. I mean . . . about you. . . .'

She faltered and stopped. The eager glow faded from her eyes, and a look of bewilderment took its place and then gave way to anguish as she realized that Estelle's mind was not on what she was saying.

She was not listening. . . .

She was not listening. She hadn't heard. She was standing there, but her mind wasn't there . . . her mind was somewhere else, somewhere far away. She hadn't heard anything . . . not properly.

In the silence, Estelle came to herself and struggled to find suitable words.

'I . . . that's wonderful, Julia,' she said, 'I'm—I'm so glad. I told you that you could be good at anything you put your mind to. I . . .'

She broke off helplessly, turned and walked to the window. Swinging round to look at Julia, she made up her mind suddenly that here, now, she would break her news; she would make her first farewell. Julia would tell the others when she went home—she herself would telephone to Nicholas—now, as soon as Julia left—and she would ask him to come and see her . . . and tell him before he could hear it from anybody else. It had to come. This was the beginning.

'Julia, I've something to tell you, too,' she said. 'It's—it's quite important news, and I hope it'll make you as happy as—as it has made me.'

'Yes, Miss Dryden?' No, she hadn't heard. She'd been thinking about this.

'I'm going to be married—to Mr. Hermann.'

The unexpectedness of the announcement, the effort to understand what she had heard and, understanding, to judge its full import, kept Julia speechless. She had no words. Then congratulations came to her lips and she uttered them awkwardly and after that the silence fell and lengthened. In the stillness, Estelle saw the colour receding from her face, leaving it chalk-white.

'You'll be . . . that means you'll have to go away, doesn't it?'

'Yes, Julia.'

'When?'

'Very soon, I'm afraid. Almost at . . . at once.'

'Will you . . . I suppose you'll come back . . . on visits?'

'Yes. Yes, I—of course I shall.'

Julia looked slowly down at her hands, screened by the edge of the table. The paper she was holding was crushed into a tight, moist ball. The gay scarlet ribbon had fallen off and now lay on the carpet, its bow still tied, its edges faintly spotted with ink.

She looked up and smiled at Estelle.

'I'm awfully glad, Miss Dryden,' she said. 'I—I think I must go now, if you don't mind, because I—I'm rather late. You'll be coming to Wood Mount . . . will you?'

'I may be, Julia.'

'Good-bye, Miss Dryden.'

'Good-bye, Julia.'

Julia went outside and shut the door quietly behind her. She went out of the house, out of the gate, skirted the main road and climbed a gate into a field. She walked swiftly along the well-known short cuts to Wood Mount. The noise of the street, of the town fell behind and died away; in the silence of the green fields she walked homeward, her mind empty, her eyes fixed ahead. Somewhere along the way, she remembered her satchel in the hall of the Red House and her bicycle at the shop of Mr. Brett, but she did not pause and did not turn. Somewhere along the way she stopped to tear the poem slowly across and across again and yet again and drop the pieces into a sluggish little stream. Nobody saw her as she reached home and went into the hall of Wood Mount. She walked up the stairs and into her room and closed the door behind her.

*   *   *

It was almost half-past five. Nicholas sorted the papers on his desk, walked across to the filing cabinet and had placed them all into the appropriate folders when he heard somebody come into the office. Turning, he saw Cliff Hermann, standing in the doorway. He filed the last paper with meticulous care.

'Hello,' he said.

'Can I talk to you for a minute or two?' asked Cliff.

For a few moments, Nicholas felt nothing but a steady drumming in his ears. He forced himself to nod coolly at the other man, and indicated a chair.

'Sit down,' he said.

'No, thanks. No, I won't sit down,' said Cliff. 'What I've come to say won't take long—and I'm sorry I'm here and I'm sorry I've got to say it.' He waited for a moment and then: 'Estelle is going to marry me,' he said.

He did not wait for a reply. Since the moment of his entrance he had not looked at Nicholas. Now he stared out across the street to Jeff's office and spoke in his low, firm tones.

'You've known for some time what I wanted,' he said. 'but I didn't know how it would end. But the end was ... she said she'd marry me. So I'm taking her away. As I see it, there's nothing to stay for—except to make her and a lot of other people unhappy. She doesn't want to leave this place. She's put down deep roots, and pulling them up is going to hurt her even more than she knows. She doesn't know I'm in here telling you this. She planned to tell you herself, this evening. She planned to speak to you herself—to you and Julia—before any of the others got to know. But I thought it over and I didn't see what could be gained by any of us by stringing this thing out. So I've told you, and now I'm going to tell her I've told you and I'm going to get her away to-night.' He faced Nicholas for the first time. 'And that's all. I said I'm sorry and I mean it. Someone besides myself was bound to love her ... to want her ... but I wish to God it hadn't happened to be you.'

He stopped speaking and turned to the door and opened it. He glanced back briefly at the man standing with a still, white expressionless face in the middle of the room. He felt a hundred years old, and tired and bitter and drained. It hadn't been a fight. It had been a walk-over—and so long as he lived, he would remember what he had done to this man and to his sister Julia.

The door closed behind him. Nicholas did not move. On the empty, tidy table the telephone began to ring and he turned slowly and listened to it—and let it go on ringing. . . .

CHAPTER SEVENTEEN

CLIFF left Nicholas in the office and went swiftly to the Red House and into the drawing-room. It was empty. He walked out into the hall once more and then, looking into the dining-room, saw Estelle standing by the window. He went in, took her into his arms and spoke quickly and firmly.

'Estelle—you're coming away with me—now. To-night.'

She stared up at him and he went on without waiting for her to speak.

'I've told Roselle; she saw us in the Nursing Home to-day, and so she didn't really have to be told. She knows. And Nicholas knows.'

'Nicholas. . . .'

'He knows. I told him myself—just now. I went to his office and I told him, and it's over and it was the only way to do it. It's done and there's no reason for you to stay here giving out the news piecemeal and tearing yourself—tearing us both to pieces. I've cabled Robert. You've got to get your things together now, and I'll call for you as soon as I've cleared up my own things at The George. We'll be married in London and we'll take the first two seats they can offer us on a plane to New York. And from there you can go on and choose a piece of land somewhere out in green country and I'll build you a house on it and we'll live there and be happy and raise kids and forget the Waynes and Greenhurst for a little while. No—don't say anything. This is the only way, and you've got to believe that. And now start packing; you haven't a lot of time.'

She freed herself and looked at him.

'Julia——' she began.

'Nicholas will tell Julia. She's coming to see you this evening. She's bringing you a poem. If you're wise and if you want to save her a lot of heartache, you'll——'

'She came,' said Estelle.

'Julia?'

'Yes. She was late going home from school and she wanted
to tell me about her having won the poetry prize.'

The poetry prize. *Spun Gold* . . . She would have copied it
out. She would have rolled it up and tied it with ribbon and
brought it as Long John brought his treasures to lay them at
Simon's feet.

'I knew she was coming,' he said, slowly, 'but I thought, I'd
. . . I hoped I'd just be in time to——' He broke off. 'Where's
the poem?'

'The——?'

'The poem. *Spun Gold*. Where is it?'

'She didn't bring the poem,' said Estelle. 'She only came to
tell me that she had won the poetry prize—but while she was
telling me, Cliff, I . . . suddenly I made up my mind to tell her,
and so I did.'

There was a long silence.

'What did she say?' asked Cliff, at last.

Estelle put her head against him with a sigh, and he tightened his arms round her and held her close.

'She didn't say much,' she said. 'She went away.'

'She didn't give you anything, bring you anything?'

'No. I thought she was holding something, but she didn't
give it to me.'

Spun Gold. . . .

On the carpet by the table, Cliff saw a bright thread of
colour, and his eyes stayed on it for long moments.

Scarlet ribbon to bind it. And she had crushed it in her
hands and taken it away. . . .

Julia. . . .

Perhaps, he thought desperately, there were special angels in
Heaven who flew down and patched up little girls' hearts.

*   *   *

It was Paul who walked with Julia across the fields to
Templeby. That she was in trouble, he had no doubt. That she

would prefer to be left unquestioned, he was even more certain —and so he said nothing.

She had not wanted to come. Miss Cornhill had looked at her, drawn her own conclusions and said nothing. It was Paul who spoke gently to her of the music that was to be played by Escramas, sung by Gonzalez. It was Paul who had promised to go with her; Nicholas promised to fetch her home when the concert was over.

Nicholas got to Templeby as the tumult of applause broke out to greet the appearance of the famous violinist. As the sounds died away, as the expectant hush fell, he glanced in at the row of seats near the door and his gaze rested for a moment on an empty chair.

Julia's. She might, he thought, have gone round to the back to see Paul. He would look for her after the concert.

In no mood to stay and listen to the music, he turned and walked slowly out on to the empty terrace. He went over to a far corner and stood staring into the darkness, his thoughts heavy with misery.

It was over. Somewhere deep within him he felt the stirring of something that might be relief. The suspense, the agony of waiting—so much at least was behind him. Before him, at this moment, he saw nothing but pain and emptiness—and loneliness.

He heard the first notes of the violin, and his mouth twisted in a grim smile. That was all it needed, he thought jeeringly. Night—and heartbreak—and a violin playing. A fitting end to a rustic interlude.

But for all his jeering, he knew that the sound of the violin was almost more than he could bear. Not to-night. . . .

He moved restlessly, and saw a shadow fall across the lighted doorway. A figure came out on to the terrace, and Nicholas had no need to ask who it was.

Estelle walked towards the deep shadows at the end of the terrace, and then hesitated.

'Nicholas,' she called, softly.

He turned. She could not see his face, but she could picture it clearly enough; she knew its every line, every curve, every expression.

'Nicholas'—she went forward until she was standing beside him, and began to speak in a low, quick tone—'Nicholas, I couldn't go without . . . without seeing you. I thought I could. I thought I should—but I—I couldn't. I wanted so much to see you and to say good-bye and . . . and thank you, oh, thank you with all my heart and . . .'

'All your heart?'

'From the bottom of my heart. I loved you, Nicholas, but it was never——'

'Never quite enough.'

'Will you say good-bye?'

'Good-bye, Estelle.' His voice was quiet. 'And . . . thank you for coming.'

She stood still and, for a shaking moment, saw clearly for the first time all that she was leaving. The quiet shores of her childhood, her girlhood were receding. She was going—to what? She did not know. The man, the land, the life—all were unknown; all she could be certain of was the force which was driving her.

It was over. There was nothing to stay for.

She turned and walked swiftly away. She left the dim terrace, the great lighted house and made her way out to the forecourt and to the car in which Cliff awaited her. He did not speak as he drove away. He let her weep quietly against him, and stared straight before him at the road, thinking of Nicholas Wayne and of what he was taking from him.

*   *   *

Nicholas went slowly down the steps into the garden; the music grew fainter. There was grass under his feet; the arms of the magnificent beech trees rose far above his head. He stopped beside one of the great trunks and leaned against it to get ease from the pain that gripped him. The music was a sigh

, far away; all around him was darkness and loneliness.

And then he heard a faint movement, and waited to hear it
ain. A bird, perhaps, in the branches; or a small animal
sturbed.

The sound was repeated—a stirring in the darkness some-
ere near him. He took a step forward and at first saw
thing—and then he looked down at his feet and saw Julia.

She was lying prone on the grass, and when he spoke her
me she rose slowly and stiffly to her feet and stood beside
n. Though he could not see her face, he knew that her grief,
e his own, was tearless.

'You oughtn't to be here,' he said gently.

'No.'

There was a pause. He could find nothing to say to her.
en he heard the strained young voice.

'She . . . she's gone, hasn't she?'

'Yes, Julia. She's gone.'

'I . . . I suppose she'll be . . . awfully happy?'

'Yes. She'll be very happy.'

That was all. She turned towards the house and seemed for
ew moments to be listening to the strains of the distant
lin. Then a small hand came out, groping, and Nicholas
k it in his own and held it tightly and protectively.

'Nicholas. . . .'

She turned to gaze at the thick woods that marked the site
Wood Mount, and Nicholas, following her glance, seemed
see the gracious white house waiting.

'Let's go home, shall we?' he said, gently.

'Yes.' Julia's cold hand seemed to warm a little in his own.
t's go home.'

They walked together towards the distant rise, hand in
d.

The Blue Sky of Spring

is the second of Elizabeth Cadell's trio of lovable and witty novels about the Waynes of Wood Mount, Greenhurst. The others are THE LARK SHALL SING and SIX IMPOSSIBLE THINGS.

he Lark Shall Sing

ere was no money, the family was scattered, and
cille, who had mothered them all since she was
teen, had thoughts of marrying. The sensible thing to
 would have been to sell the house, but the family
d different ideas. Rushing back from their jobs, from
ir schools, bringing with them an odd assortment of
nds, they tried to convince her that the house must
 kept. This wasn't all, for a film star made Lucille
nder whether her fiancé was not too staid and
sible.

ix Impossible Things

holas Wayne, like Alice in Wonderland, finds it hard
believe impossible things: to believe that he could
jet Estelle Dryden who went to America ten years
 or that his sister Julia, who had always been a
ggy child, should come back from Rome tall and
active with a supple figure and delicate auburn hair.
 after a good deal of plain speaking from a pretty
man, Nicholas is obliged to change his mind.

OTHER ROMANTIC NOVELS BY
ELIZABETH CADELL

All these books are available at your bookshop or newsagent *can be ordered direct from the publisher. Just tick the titles you w and fill in the form below.*

CORONET BOOKS, Cash Sales Department, Kernick Indus
Estate, Penryn, Cornwall.

Please send cheque or postal order. No currency, and allow
following for postage and packing:

1 book—7p per copy, 2–4 books—5p per copy, 5–8 books—4p
copy, 9–15 books—2½p per copy, 16–30 books—2p per cop
U.K., 7p per copy overseas.

Name...

Address..

....